LAST
ORGY
OF THE
DIVINE
HERMIT

LAST
ORGY
OF THE
DIVINE
HERMIT

*MARK
LEYNER*

Little, Brown and Company
New York Boston London

Copyright © 2021 by Mark Leyner

Little, Brown and Company
Hachette Book Group
1290 Avenue of the Americas, New York, NY 10104
littlebrown.com

First Edition: January 2021

Little, Brown and Company is a division of Hachette Book Group, Inc. The Little, Brown name and logo are trademarks of Hachette Book Group, Inc.

The publisher is not responsible for websites (or their content) that are not owned by the publisher.

The Hachette Speakers Bureau provides a wide range of authors for speaking events. To find out more, go to hachettespeakersbureau.com or call (866) 376-6591.

ISBN 978-0-316-56050-4
LCCN 2020946024

Printing 1, 2020

LSC-C

Printed in the United States of America

LAST
ORGY
OF THE
DIVINE
HERMIT

Introduction

E

F P

T O Z

L P E D

P E C F D

E D F C Z P

F E L O P Z D

D E F P O T E C

L E F O D P C T

F D P L T C E O

P E Z O L C F T D

PATIENT

*(looking through the phoropter lenses
and reading from the eye chart)*

"The first orgasm I ever had was so intense I separated both my shoulders and shit in my pants."

So begins *Last Orgy of the Divine Hermit*…

The OPTOMETRIST *switches lenses on the phoropter.*

OPTOMETRIST

Is this any better? Sharper?

PATIENT

Oh my god! I wasn't even close!

OPTOMETRIST

That's OK. Can you read it for me now?

The PATIENT *absently twirls a lock of hair around her finger as she reads through the device, which completely masks her face—*

PATIENT

"On June 26, 2035, Kermunkachunk, the capital of Chalazia, was engulfed in chaos. The Chalazian Mafia Faction, a fanatical offshoot of the Chalazian Children's Theater, had

7

assumed control of the city center and was carrying out mass executions. Enemies, real and especially imagined, were dragged out of their office buildings and gutted in the street."

So begins *Last Orgy of the Divine Hermit*...

OPTOMETRIST

Excellent. Now, this makes it blurry, yes?

PATIENT

Yes.

OPTOMETRIST

Is it better like this...or like this? One...or two?

PATIENT

About the same.

OPTOMETRIST

OK. Now, can you read this?

PATIENT

So begins *Last Orgy of the Divine Hermit*, in which a father and his daughter, in Chalazia researching an ethnography of the unique criminal subculture of the Chalazian Mafia Faction, spend a night at the Bar Pulpo, Kermunkachunk's #1 spoken-word karaoke bar, where seemingly extemporaneous conversations are, in actuality, being read from multiple karaoke screens arrayed around the barroom. Moreover, it's

Thursday—*Father/Daughter Nite*—when the bar is fre-
quented by actual fathers and daughters, as well as couples
role-playing fathers and daughters.

OPTOMETRIST

Good. Now…can you make out any of this line? I know it's small.

PATIENT

Not really. I'm guessing here…Uh…

fneixa alsdfy hoypm ewrse dnfbmoldfh vusyvjfg nktoinb
xzinkhg

…I'm not really sure.

OPTOMETRIST

Alright, give me just a moment here…

He makes a quick note on the PATIENT's *chart and again switches lenses on
the phoropter—*

OPTOMETRIST

How about now? Can you make out anything?

PATIENT

Meanwhile, outside on the
piazza, sub-factions of the
Chalazian Mafia Faction vie
for supremacy in a

PATIENT

Meanwhile, outside on the
piazza, sub-factions of the
Chalazian Mafia Faction vie
for supremacy in a

never-ending frenzy of
stomach-churning savagery.
Chalazian Mafia Faction
street soldiers commit acts of
unimaginable sadism,
reveling in carnage and the
grotesque mutilation of their
victims' corpses. But it's
worth keeping in mind that
these are kids who, several
years ago, frequently only
several *weeks* ago (several
days ago, in some cases), were
prancing around onstage in a
Chalazian Children's
Theater production of *Clever
Jack and the Magic Beanstalk.*
These are young people
who've traded their
exuberant devotion to
musical theater for an
irrepressible desire to kill and
be killed out on the piazza.
Histrionic narcissists to the
core, Chalazian Mafia
Faction street soldiers
pirouette as they die, like
defecating dogs aligning
themselves to the earth's
electromagnetic field. These
ex-musical-theater kids are

never-ending frenzy of
stomach-churning savagery.
Chalazian Mafia Faction
street soldiers commit acts of
unimaginable sadism,
reveling in carnage and the
grotesque mutilation of their
victims' corpses. But it's
worth keeping in mind that
these are kids who, several
years ago, frequently only
several *weeks* ago (several
days ago, in some cases), were
prancing around onstage in a
Chalazian Children's
Theater production of *Clever
Jack and the Magic Beanstalk.*
These are young people
who've traded their
exuberant devotion to
musical theater for an
irrepressible desire to kill and
be killed out on the piazza.
Histrionic narcissists to the
core, Chalazian Mafia
Faction street soldiers
pirouette as they die, like
defecating dogs aligning
themselves to the earth's
electromagnetic field. These
ex-musical-theater kids are

LAST ORGY OF THE DIVINE HERMIT

always "on," always performing for the CCTV cameras that ring the perimeter of the piazza. The Chalazian Mafia Faction, we're told, is like a combination of the Gambino crime family and the Khmer Rouge. Proclaiming itself to be "against everything and everyone," it is necessarily, per its own ethos, riven by internecine conflict, hence this chaotic, blood-drenched phantasmagoria—this unspeakable orgy of violence—that ensues without respite, day in and day out, on the piazza outside the Bar Pulpo, Kermunkachunk's #1 spoken-word karaoke bar.

OPTOMETRIST

Now, you're seeing two columns of text, side by side, yes?

PATIENT

Yes.

always "on," always performing for the CCTV cameras that ring the perimeter of the piazza. The Chalazian Mafia Faction, we're told, is like a combination of the Gambino crime family and the Khmer Rouge. Proclaiming itself to be "against everything and everyone," it is necessarily, per its own ethos, riven by internecine conflict, hence this chaotic, blood-drenched phantasmagoria—this unspeakable orgy of violence—that ensues without respite, day in and day out, on the piazza outside the Bar Pulpo, Kermunkachunk's #1 spoken-word karaoke bar.

OPTOMETRIST

Now, you're seeing two columns of text, side by side, yes?

PATIENT

Yes.

OPTOMETRIST

OK…Let me know when they've merged into one column.

OPTOMETRIST

OK…Let me know when they've merged into one column.

PATIENT

Uh…

PATIENT

Uh…

PATIENT

…now.

OPTOMETRIST

Good. Now, can you read that for me or is it too blurry?

PATIENT

No, I can read it:

> Meanwhile, outside on the piazza, sub-factions of the Chalazian Mafia Faction vie for supremacy in a never-ending frenzy of stomach-churning savagery. Chalazian Mafia Faction street soldiers commit acts of unimaginable sadism, reveling in carnage and the grotesque mutilation of their victims' corpses. But it's worth keeping in mind that these are kids who, several years ago, frequently only several *weeks* ago (several *days* ago, in some cases), were prancing around onstage in a Chalazian Children's Theater production of *Clever Jack and the Magic Beanstalk.* These are young people who've traded their exuberant devotion to musical theater for an irrepressible desire to kill and be killed out on the piazza. Histrionic

narcissists to the core, Chalazian Mafia Faction street soldiers pirouette as they die, like defecating dogs aligning themselves to the earth's electromagnetic field. These ex-musical-theater kids are always "on," always performing for the CCTV cameras that ring the perimeter of the piazza. The Chalazian Mafia Faction, we're told, is like a combination of the Gambino crime family and the Khmer Rouge. Proclaiming itself to be "against everything and everyone," it is necessarily, per its own ethos, riven by internecine conflict, hence this chaotic, blood-drenched phantasmagoria—this unspeakable orgy of violence—that ensues without respite, day in and day out, on the piazza outside the Bar Pulpo, Kermunkachunk's #1 spoken-word karaoke bar...

The PATIENT *stops reading...*

PATIENT

Keep going?

OPTOMETRIST

Please.

PATIENT

Chalazia is a tiny country wedged between Moldova and Romania, though recognized by neither. Almost every surface in Chalazia (actually, *every* surface) tests positive for traces of cocaine. The entirety of the country is cordoned off with yellow crime scene tape, all 148 kilometers of border, a phenomenon visible from outer space. (In actuality a Neolithic geoglyph akin to the Kazakh Steppe earthworks or the more recent Nazca Lines, this cordon was made by removing the top layer of the bluish-white reflecting salt flats [that once covered all of Chalazia] to reveal a bright yellow subsoil.) An elaborate system of sewers (now in complete disuse) descends some 1,800 kilometers beneath the ground, ramifying across the subterranean latitudes of the entire planet—a feat of engineering that many believe could only have been achieved by corrupt ancient aliens. (Even in 800 B.C., the Chalazian construction and waste-carting industries were rife with racketeering.) These ancient sewers make Chalazia both the farthest and the nearest destination from any point of origin on earth. In other words, at any given moment, Chalazia may be wedged between any two other nations. Fossilized ancient Chalazian shit—coprolites—can today be found almost anywhere. Anywhere, actually. And everywhere. Apropos of which, a previous incarnation of the Bar Pulpo was called the "Coprocabana" (which was obviously not a spoken-word karaoke bar).

The Chalazian *joie de merde* is only surpassed by its *joie de guerre*.

But could this violence, this atrocious, unabating carnage, be as random and incoherent as it appears? Is there someone responsible for orchestrating the perpetual conflagration on the piazza outside the Bar Pulpo—the piazza, with its stench of sweat, lube, and gasoline, littered with shell casings, cigarette butts, and used condoms floating in puddles of blood?

Perhaps it's the Divine Hermits themselves, those heretical holy men, who are the real puppet masters, the ones calling the shots on the brazen predation that's come to define contemporary Kermunkachunk. Like Kabbalistic tzaddiks or Shaiva tantrikas but historically associated with the Chalazian Mafia Faction, these antinomian mystics, moonlighting as Mafia warlords, combine the esoteric pursuit of nondualistic illumination with extortion and loan-sharking. *Last Orgy of the Divine Hermit* makes a strong case that it's these eponymous individuals who are masterminding events on the piazza from their perch in the Floating Casino on Lake Little Lake, where these racketeering illuminati who wear their diamond-encrusted hair balls and engraved prostates around their necks as amulets, these shirtless recluses with their white chest hair and neon-orange nylon sweatpants, paradoxically socialize every Thursday night.

Made members (and frequently godfathers) of the Chalazian Mafia Faction, these adepts remain literally above the fray, levitating a foot or two above their seats as they play a traditional Chalazian game that combines Scrabble and mahjong. They roll their eyes at the suggestion that they have anything to do with the violence on the piazza, let alone direct it, as, seemingly in a trance, they endlessly shuffle their tiles (this is known as "permutation of the letters"). And they send deeply encrypted death threats to anyone with the temerity to suggest that they encrypt their death threats.

The Chalazian Mafia Faction warlord and the Divine Hermit embody (frequently within the same individual) two complementary modalities: criminality and *devequt* (cleaving to the divine), encapsulating, within this single chimerical figure, the Chalazian concept of human existence. As for the CMF street soldiers themselves, when it comes to fashioning weapons, they are remarkably resourceful, and have been known to make shanks out of soft-serve ice cream.

The men's room in the Bar Pulpo is an insane parody of the ladies' room. It is haunted by the anthropoid ghosts of the ancient aliens (the *Kermunks*) who built the vast, labyrinthine sewer system. In this particular men's room (in *any* men's room, actually) we encounter "misshapen forms of the gods in agony." This men's room is, in a sense, like an incubator, where the larval Divine Hermits molt and mature, sheltered from predators and fed by the mechanomorphic vermin that scurry behind the toilets. It is this men's room from which, in a sense, they migrate on deciduous wings to the Floating Casino. And it is where, at the end of his life, the Divine Hermit instinctively returns, where he and his demonic double, the Mafia warlord, are locked in a reciprocal interrogation in a mirror above the sink—"the mirror from which there is no escape." It is where Ron Howard looks in the mirror and sees Clint Howard. (Sixty years ago, on an episode of *Bonanza*, Clint Howard, in blackface, played a little African boy who brings the Ebola virus to the Ponderosa, sparking two consecutive three-day weekends of deadly pogroms that eventually became known as the Coachella Valley Music and Arts Festival.)

OPTOMETRIST

Close enough.

He changes lenses on the phoropter.

OPTOMETRIST

Now, can you make out any of this?

PATIENT

(squinting through the phoropter)

Some.

OPTOMETRIST

Give it a try.

PATIENT

And the Chalazian *joie de guerre* is only surpassed by its *joie de lire.*

Among the most literate people on earth, Chalazians almost never read in solitude or silence, only publicly and out loud ("belting"), either from the spoken-word karaoke screens or, swaying back and forth, from the Big-Character Posters that festoon the perimeter of the piazza, and whereas these collective performances are widely referred to as "orgiastic," the more cosmopolitan Kermunkachunkians (the "Kermunkachunkian cognoscenti," the most zealous of whom are, of course, the street soldiers of the CMF) go one step further, stigmatizing solitary reading as "prurient and petit bourgeois," i.e., a mortal sin akin to eating your own earwax...

I'm sorry—

...*one's* own earwax.

OPTOMETRIST

Excellent!

PATIENT

When, at the beginning of *Last Orgy of the Divine Hermit,* the door to the Bar Pulpo opens on Father/Daughter Nite, the babble (which, to an untutored ear, wouldn't sound much different from the ambient hubbub of any bar) includes the drunken voices of an anthropologist and his daughter (Gaby, a gorgeous, young neo-structural filmmaker from New York) who are in Kermunkachunk researching an ethnography about the ultraviolent Chalazian Mafia Faction, the two of them seated in a booth across from each other and reading aloud, along with everyone else, from the numerous spoken-word karaoke screens, Chalazia's most beloved folktale, which is sometimes palindromically called "Nite of the Daughter's Father."

This story of a mortally ill father and his beloved daughter in an inn or tavern (of the sort traditionally habituated by itinerant tradesmen, grizzled sailors on weeklong benders, crossing guards in heavy mascara and fluorescent-yellow vests, etc.), this story which culminates in the father's staggering Dance of Death, is the foundational narrative in Chalazian culture. All the ontological and epistemological preoccupations that constitute the Chalazian mentalité are encoded within this one folktale (and its innumerable variants), which is why, one assumes, the author and his daughter have, on this particular "nite," ensconced themselves at the Bar Pulpo, itself a *matryoshka* nesting of successfully smaller and more sacred spaces — the barroom, the men's room, the stall.

One of the first things you'll see upon arriving at Kermunka-chunk International Airport are the huge murals depicting various scenes from the folktale. Running the entire length of the moving walkway that conveys you from the arrival gates to the baggage carousels, these monumental murals, unlike the Snellen chart, are read from right to left:

- The father and the daughter toasting their everlasting devotion to each other, clinking tiny tin mugs (rough-hewn shot glasses) of "gravy," a fiery Chalazian vermifuge, washed down with flagons of lager.
- The daughter pensively blowing thick white smoke rings which settle around her father's neck like an Elizabethan ruff, as he regales her with an account of the marionette show he'd chanced upon that afternoon.
- Their final embrace and heartrending goodbye, the mere allusion to which can reduce the most hardened, remorseless CMF street assassins to sobbing hysterics.
- The father's drunken stagger from the men's room, his Dance of Death. This is the critical inflection point in the folktale when the father gazes into the mirror above the sink, provoking a strobe-like seizure of initiatory transfigurations (in sober moments, simply the palimpsest that is one's reflection), and emerges to perform his lurching *Danse Macabre*, his *Totentanz* (and/or actually dying, depending on the variant). It's a raw, contorted, convulsive improvisation, and yet, at the same time, highly…uh…highly…*caramelized*?

The OPTOMETRIST *changes lenses in the phoropter.*

OPTOMETRIST

Try it now.

PATIENT

It's a raw, contorted, convulsive improvisation, and yet, at the same time, highly ritualized…

Ah, *ritualized*!

OPTOMETRIST

(laughing)

Ritualized. Caramelized. Same difference.

PATIENT

It's a raw, contorted, convulsive improvisation, and yet, at the same time, highly ritualized, hieratic...very Butoh.

OPTOMETRIST

Excellent.

PATIENT

Don't Let This Robot Suck Your Dick Productions, Kermunkachunk's most prestigious film and television production company, is responsible for innumerable movies and miniseries based on the folktale, both live-action and animated.

The company's ethos, their *cri de guerre*, really—shouted by a robot at the beginning of each movie like the roar of the MGM lion—was taken from a commercial for International Delight coffee creamers: "I like it international and I expect to be delighted!"

There are, by now, thousands of variants of "Nite of the Daughter's Father," each a cryptographic hash of the previous iteration, many of which, at this point, don't even include a father or a daughter or take place at "nite," but the standard version, the ur-folktale, takes place "a long time ago, farther back than anyone can remember..."

There was once a small inn at the foot of a hollow mountain, a hollow mountain that was said to be inhabited by a race of warlike elves (although these warlike elves have nothing to do with this story!). One evening, as rain poured down from the skies and, driven by the wind, pelted the windows of the inn, in walked a stooped and jaundiced old watchmaker, gripping his coat's lapels and shaking the wetness onto the wooden plank floor. He hung the coat up on a peg on the wall and sat, exhausted, at a round, rough-hewn table. Several days before, he'd been to see the physician, an elderly man decades older than the old watchmaker himself. "You're very sick," the wizened sage had told him after a careful examination. "You have late-stage cirrhosis of the liver"—a glaringly anachronistic, *avant la lettre* diagnosis, arrived at through an assortment of fuming alembics, strange alchemical assays, and *tzeruf,* the permutation of letters. "You're dying," he averred solemnly, "and another drink will kill you even sooner than that!" Nevertheless, on this very evening, the old watchmaker signaled to the barmaid, wiggling two fingers, and she brought him two tiny tin mugs of "gravy," which he knocked back in rapid succession. Just then, a young woman, mid-twenties, petite, and soigné in her hooded cloak, entered and surveyed the bar. The watchmaker waved, catching her attention, and beckoned her over to the table. It was his beloved and kindhearted daughter whom he adored more than anything in this world. He'd arranged to meet her here at this inn at the foot of a hollow mountain to tell her the sad news about his illness, to tell her that he was dying. And although she had traveled miles and miles in an ox-drawn cart along rock-strewn, muddy roads in the raging storm and was completely exhausted, she happily threw her arms around him and kissed him over and over again, before removing the hood of her cloak, dappled from the rain, to reveal her lustrous black hair intricately plaited into a chignon that rested at the nape of her neck. He was her beloved and kindhearted father and she adored *him* more than anything in the world.

On cold nights, when she was young, he would hold her little feet in his hands to warm them as he sang:

> You are my sweet sweet girl
> And I love you so.
> This song will last forever
> Long long after I go.

The PATIENT *chokes up, memories triggered of her own dad, now deceased, singing tenderly to her when* she *was little.*

OPTOMETRIST

Are you OK? Do you need a minute?

PATIENT

(takes a deep breath, exhales)

I'm good.

(she resumes, this time giving the words a melody)

> You are my sweet sweet girl
> And I love you so.

This song will last forever
Long long after I go.

The old watchmaker and his daughter clinked their shot glasses of gravy, toasting their everlasting devotion to each other. They reminisced and gossiped and laughed, the father buying time before he was forced to deliver the terrible news to his sweet girl, who tilted her head and gazed at him, her eyes and smile shining bright and wide with loving admiration and solicitude.

"So, what did the physician—that ancient mountebank—say?" the daughter asked, fidgeting with some soggy cardboard coaster on the table and pursing her lips nervously.

Now the watchmaker took a deep breath…

"Everything's perfectly fine," he lied. "I'm in robust health."

The prospect of inflicting upon her the grim news of his dire condition overwhelmed him with dread. He was incapable of saying or doing anything that might hurt her or make her sad. He simply couldn't bring himself to do it.

She shut her eyes and exhaled, her face slackening with relief.

"Oh Father, I was so worried," she said, tears welling in her eyes. "That's the most wonderful news to hear!"

She reached across the table and held his cold hands in hers to warm them.

Looking at her keen, happy face, the old watchmaker felt terribly guilty. Withholding the truth from her was so antithetical to the openheartedness and candor of their relationship. She would feel such a profound sense of betrayal knowing that he hadn't confided in her, that he'd allowed her to be so blindsided, left her so vulnerable, so cruelly unprepared for the shock of his impending death. Each time, though, that he thought he'd sufficiently girded himself to reveal what the physician had actually said, his resolve would disintegrate, that lump in his throat would rise, blocking the words from coming out. But just as he'd given up, hanging his head with the shame of his own abject cowardice, everything suddenly fell into place as if the inner workings of one of his watches, scattered in disarray upon his work table — all the tiny gears and springs — had spontaneously arranged themselves into the intricate movement of a timepiece. There *was* a way of sparing her, of telling the truth that wouldn't be so excruciatingly painful. Resorting to a sort of sleight of hand, he would convey this dreadful news obliquely, by way of an allegory.

"I chanced upon the most marvelous marionette show on the way to the inn," said the old watchmaker.

"Oh, how charming, Father!" said his daughter. "Tell me, what was the show about?"

Now he could unreservedly express how deeply, how completely, how *exquisitely* he loved her...and say goodbye.

And thus began the watchmaker's vivid, extended, and increasingly intoxicated re-creation of the tale enacted by the marionettes, a tale from an even more remote, primeval time, a tale which was called *La Muñeca de la Mafia Chalazian* ("Baby Doll of the Chalazian Mafia"):

There was once a great and fearsome warlord known all over Chalazia for his ruthless ferocity, cunning, noble magnanimity, and the breadth of his esoteric wisdom. He had a daughter, his only heir, whom he adored and cherished beyond anyone and anything. She was a brilliant young woman, and beautiful besides. So she had hundreds of suitors. But she devoted herself most conscientiously to counseling her father about the internecine complexities of his vocation, which was, of course, both felonious *and* philanthropic. Knowing that her father would never allow her to participate in his "business," she disguised herself as a typical henchman, becoming her father's most trusted advisor (his *consigliere*, in other words).

The day came when the father, suffering from hereditary Creutzfeldt-Jakob disease (a degenerative and fatal neurological prion disease, akin to bovine spongiform encephalopathy and afflicting most Chalazian men late in life), knew he was dying and called his daughter to his bedside. Blind, racked by myoclonic jerks and twitches, and able only to gasp and whisper, he drew her close and said, "I've known all along that it was you giving me such shrewd advice. Who else but my own beloved daughter could have been so wise, so selfless and loyal?" He bestowed upon her the title *La Muñeca de la Mafia Chalazian* and bequeathed to her his legacy of exotic riches, material and mystical. "Be careful, my dearest one, that the man you marry loves *you* and does not simply covet all that I've worked so tirelessly to amass." And with that he took his final breath and perished.

The daughter went on to become the most powerful woman ever to reign over a criminal enterprise, the organization under her command soon orders of magnitude vaster than her father's had ever been.

And who do you think she married from among the hundreds of handsome but conniving young suitors who'd sought her hand? None of them!

She married the effete little gnome who lived under the ground in a deep well who had frequently disguised himself as the warlord's daughter to facilitate the real daughter's dissimulation.

In fact, at their wedding, they dressed as each other. A custom that still prevails in Chalazia to this day!

"And just as the curtain fell, the storm began," said the old watchmaker upon finally concluding this drama of a dying warlord and his daughter's patrimony, his rendition taking well over two hours and considerably more embellished, convoluted, and drunkenly digressive, and including, as it did, his uncanny mimicry of the speech patterns and gesticulations of each and every character, major and minor.

"And you should have seen how comical it was," he continued, "when all these marvelous marionettes tried to scurry off under their own power, without the help of the puppeteers, who'd abandoned them onstage to seek shelter from the deluge!"

And then, upon further consideration of the plight of these frantic, crippled puppets, he added, "I suppose it was a bit sad too."

Perhaps his daughter wasn't consciously aware of what he was conveying to her at that very moment, through this tale of the fervently devoted relationship between a powerful, ailing father and his only heir, his cherished, indomitable girl (his *muñeca,* his "little doll"), to whom, on his deathbed, in the play's anguished tearjerker of a finale, he bequeaths his vast criminal empire. But the old watchmaker was confident that someday after his death, his daughter would think back and say to herself, "He told me. In his gentle, caring, oblique, and allegorical way, he told me *everything* that last night."

The marionette play, as recounted by the old watchmaker, features two stock characters of late-medieval folklore: the Chalazian Mafia Godfather, a combination of *shtarker* and *tzaddik,* of thug and holy man, fusing within himself the ruthlessness of the transnational gangster warlord and the atemporality of the eremitic mystic in the forest, who is traditionally represented as sleeping beneath portraits of Meyer Lansky and the Baal Shem Tov. He, in turn, dotes indefatigably on his daughter—the gorgeous young woman in her mid-twenties, her lustrous black hair in a plaited chignon, who is chaste, introspective, aloof, fearless, blessed with extraordinary mixed martial arts skills, a devotee of Dadaist poetry and the Japanese koto, and fanatically loyal to her father.

Such was the strange evolution of gently smiling holy men and the cunning, vindictive hoodlums who protected them and did their bidding into hybrids of both, and such is the strange milieu that is Chalazia today.

As he recounted the marionette play, the old watchmaker was drinking relentlessly, furiously, opening his throat like a marathon runner at a hydration station, gulping double gravy after double gravy and then hurling himself back into the narrative. And whereas one might think that the mind-boggling amount of alcohol he was consuming would, if not completely disable his capacity to continue, at the very least result in the sort of monotonous, repetitive, sophomoric, ultimately incoherent drivel you'd expect, it did not. To the contrary. Acting almost like a magical potion, the gravy had somehow rejuvenated him for the rigors of this fabulation (we can't help but wonder if there was even an actual marionette play in the first place), and steeled his determination to bestow this allegory upon his daughter, in all its loving plenitude and with its scrupulously encoded message. Yes, the histrionics became somewhat amped up, the syntax a bit sloppier, the perspective more kaleidoscopic, the embellishments ever more baroque—but somehow the alcohol acted like a drawing salve that extracted and put at his disposal all the disparate emotional and psychological motifs necessary for him to synthesize this anguished aria, to speak the unspeakable to her.

Meanwhile, the inn had filled with its typical habitués: the hermits and woodsmen and sailors, the peasants and pipers, the shopkeepers, dockworkers, peddlers and cobblers, the merchants and horsemen and foot soldiers, and the fat little babies battened on smoked whitefish salad and tapioca and marzipan.

At first, outbursts of raucous laughter and profane slurs and ribald exhortations clashed with and undermined poignant moments in the watchmaker's telling. (At one point, apropos of nothing, some drunk yelled out, "Everything is spurious!") The men in the inn appeared completely indifferent, oblivious. You could never catch any of them actually listening. But then, it really did come to seem (at least, to *seem*) that these men began to constitute an audience in the sense that their collective affect (laughter, groans, sighs, etc.) appeared (or was it just coincidence?) to be in sync with tonal shifts in the watchmaker's story. Under scrutiny, this phenomenon would immediately vanish. That apparent interest, that attention seemingly directed the watchmaker's way, would, on closer inspection, reveal itself to be nothing more than the glassy gaze, the stupefied gape of another lush. Nevertheless, the fluctuating dynamics within the story did actually seem, at various junctures, to orchestrate the ambience of the room.

And so the watchmaker *finally* (again, this had, by now, taken up several hours!) reached the heart-wrenching conclusion in which the dying Chalazian godfather, succumbing after a grim, protracted battle with Familial CJD, bestows the entirety of his criminal kingdom upon his beloved, grief-stricken girl (his *muñeca*), and, with his dying breath, bids her farewell.

The bar was silent. The daughter was deeply moved, shaking her head incredulously, tears in her eyes, speechless… but the spell was soon broken when, moments later, she looked up at the large clock on the wall and realized how late it had become. She rose from the table, put on her hooded cloak, and gave her father a big long hug, a culminating reprise of her earlier relief, pausing to hold him at arm's length, and tilting her head so she could affectionately appraise him, and then hugging him once more, this time with a spontaneous jolt of ardor, triggered in ways she'd only be conscious of much later by all the potent emotional symbolism with which her father had seeded his long, assiduous reconstruction of the marionette play. And she kissed him goodbye one last time, and she departed to meet her fiancé, a handsome cavalryman with a long, keloidal dueling scar across one side of his face.

The old watchmaker knew he'd never see her again. (Can a liver "break" like a heart?)

And the tears, which fell from his jaundiced eyes and spread across the rough-hewn table, crystallized, metamorphosing into a reflective surface—a mirror which, in the middle of the night, while all the drunks "slept" in a state of suspended animation, the little elves mounted above the sink in the men's room—

The PATIENT *stops, eyes occluded, arms akimbo.*

PATIENT

There were men's rooms back then?

The OPTOMETRIST *shrugs.*

PATIENT

(again reading through the phoropter)

—and when the watchmaker entered and looked at himself, an infinite mise en abyme was generated by the reflections of the mirror in the pupils of his eyes, the specular images ricocheting back and forth at the speed of light.

And within this shaft of incandescent effervescence resides the sublime truth that we inhabit an imaginary world without meaning.

And this dazzling lucidity prompts us to either dance or die, or both dance *and* die.

And this, comrades, is "the orgy."

OPTOMETRIST

(with an upraised fist)

Yes!

PATIENT

When the old watchmaker emerged a while later, he gazed disconcertedly across the inn toward the table where they'd been sitting. He'd forgotten that his daughter had left.

He'd managed by necessity—through the extremity of his sorrow and the desperation of his love, really—to temporarily transmute the alcohol into a kind of

fortifying elixir. But now that this was no longer necessary, without the imperative of that mission (the allego-
rizing of the marionette play) which propelled him
forward by the sheer force of its exigency and which
constituted a kind of stabilizing torque, he collapsed.

The alcohol seemed to hit him with a delayed, cumulative, pent-up force, a wave of gravy, a lifetime of gravy
hit him, and literally knocked him off his feet. Or was it
his own incipient Creutzfeldt-Jakob disease (the symptoms of which he'd never acknowledged out of fear of
alarming his daughter) or the magnifying effect of both
his intoxication *and* the CJD that caused the old watchmaker to spin and fall as he did?

He struggled to stand, to walk. But his direct line from
point A to point B—from men's room to table—
shattered into a delirium of vectors. He staggered, caroming into every surface he encountered, now a human Pong
ball, erratically traversing the bar back and forth in a welter of veering zigzags, crosshatching the bar's space,
repeatedly collapsing in vertiginous pirouettes, groveling
along the floor on all fours, somehow clambering again to
his feet, lurching along another haphazard, oblique trajectory, gesticulating like an airline attendant in an effort to
navigate himself, teetering in circles, grasping for imaginary overhead handrails like a brachiating chimp, until he
impacted another table or another wall, and whirled
uncontrollably to the ground in a heap, like those for-
saken, hobbling marionettes trying to escape the storm.

He cycled through a series of ritualistic masks—a truc-
ulent scowl became a look of contemptuous hauteur and

then a coy pout and then a look of cringing chagrin, the imperturbable serenity of a beatified saint suddenly giving way to PTSD shell shock and then the panic of someone about to be immolated by a mob. He looked up from the floor, like a hard-shelled insect on its back, helpless, simpering with mortification.

It was a long, pitiable, shambolic Dance of Death…a *Danse Macabre*…some improbable version of Tatsumi Hijikata's Butoh, his "dance of total darkness."

Of course, this looked like, from one perspective, nothing more than a drunk stumbling out of a men's room and trying desperately, and without success, to maintain his balance, to stay on his feet long enough to return to his seat. But from another perspective there seemed to be a very deliberate choreography, where every action and every tilt of the head and positioning of a limb became meaningful. This was the phantasm of a body, the staging of a transubstantiation, a struggle with and rapturous capitulation to one's fate, the physical articulation of yet another allegory.

His body, to borrow the words of the dance critic Jennifer Homans, "was pitched at swerving angles; arms, legs, hips, head oriented through multiple spatial planes, his eyes sent in one direction, jaw in the other, rib cage in one direction, hips in the other. Soon the feet turned out, the line took shape, the familiar positions emerged. His movements were wide, open through the chest, with deep épaulement, but they were also torqued and knotted, the limbs working in rhythmic counterpoint."

An intricate corporeal transformation from extreme old age to youth and back again, he danced a violent, strange flamenco, his body savagely capricious in its gestures. Exuding death outward in every direction, he mimed the act of tenderly sponge-bathing the Grim Reaper — a spasm-driven gesture of the arm that would begin by heading violently in exactly the opposite direction to the sponge, before tracing a wide arc of flight in space, and then buckling in on itself to finally grasp the sponge, etc., etc.

(This is, by the way, a dance that is still performed by Chalazian fathers at the weddings of their daughters.)

And so, finally, reeling, the watchmaker braced himself against a wooden post at the far end of the inn. He gathered himself, he squinted, trying to focus his eyes, and committed to a heedless line that diagonally bisected the entire inn...and he careened — his body canted at an impossible angle — toward the spot where he and his daughter had been sitting.

And he somehow swerved backward toward that table and ended up propped upright in his chair, eyes shut, shoulders slumped, head lolling, his chin on his chest, breathing irregularly, drooling...motionless like this for some time. And then pitching forward slightly...listing slowly... slowly...until his forehead was flush against the tabletop.

And here he began mumbling what was apparently some sort of demented nonsense to himself.

Was this now the verbal apraxia of a stroke victim or simply the unintelligible gibberish of a drunk with Creutzfeldt-Jakob disease?

The PATIENT *pauses, letting the question hang in the air for a moment…*

OPTOMETRIST

The etiology is too overdetermined for a folktale to bear.

PATIENT

*(resumes reading from the Snellen chart
as she peers through the lenses of the phoropter)*

But if you listened closely, you'd realize that it wasn't unintelligible gibberish at all…

The watchmaker was murmuring those things—those most secret, intimate, and anguished things, those beseeching, prayerful things—that one murmurs aloud to oneself when one feels most exposed and ashamed and abased, and when one feels, paradoxically, that some ennobling self-transfiguration may just possibly be within reach.

And if you got *very* close, and listened *very* carefully, you could begin to discern something organizing itself, a structure developing out of all this undifferentiated pathos. And you'd think to yourself, Are we projecting all this, attributing an intentionality that isn't really there, are we just hearing what we want to hear? After all, this is a drunk who literally can't pick his head up off the table at this point. But it's true. In what we'd so misapprehended as delirious gibberish, we now began to glean what seemed like deliberate pauses and cadences…like line breaks and caesuras and meters, stanzas and refrains. And again we might wonder to ourselves if it's simply some kind of alcoholic auto-echolalia that's creating a mere semblance of verse. But that can't explain the uncanny formal ingenuity, the beauty of it.

And then there emerged something of a cross between speech and song (a "Schoenbergian *Sprechtimme!*" a tipsy blacksmith, with a long glistening beard, had the chutzpah to blurt out)…and then gradually an incipient but unmistakable melody. And again, was it simply an effect of the drunken lolling of his neck and the compression of his larynx, the slight spasms as he roused himself back into consciousness after momentarily fading off, that gave a tonal rise and fall to his voice, creating the mere appearance of a melody? But, again, no—there *was* a melody. There *were* verses and refrains. The watchmaker *was* singing—yes, a completely extemporaneous song that he was conjuring up as he went along, but a song nonetheless.

And, remarkably, the watchmaker's song was slowly taken up by the other men in the bar. First by one…then another…then several more…until they were *all* singing, each and every one of them. They were singing the watchmaker's very words, as if they all knew this song, this hymn. As if, somehow, they'd *always* known it.

And now they were almost like sailors, these grizzled ghosts, at some shipmate's wake, singing a dirge about a rudderless, mastless ship disappearing into a dark mist, or over some precipice.

And amidst these men, their faces haggard, creviced with care, flush with alcohol, singing, Breughel faces,

Hogarth faces, this motley choir, singing—each of these old fathers, each the wobbling, moribund protagonist of his own disaggregated solar system, singing, singing—the watchmaker died.

And his body, as per his wishes, was unceremoniously flung into the Landwehr Canal in Berlin, the canal into which the revolutionary martyr Rosa Luxemburg was thrown after her execution by Freikorps thugs in 1919.

And so, this is the folktale in its most unadulterated form that's read aloud from the spoken-word karaoke screens by those in attendance at the Bar Pulpo on Father/Daughter Nite.

The numerous spoken-word karaoke screens stream an array of variant versions of the folktale, which can differ wildly from one another (some fairly radical alterations to the original have been attributed to algorithmic methods like predictive text and auto-complete). Which variant a father/daughter pair reads aloud depends on where they're sitting, i.e., on their sight lines to a particular screen. But although, at any given moment, any pair is likely to be reading something entirely different from any other pair (producing the Bar Pulpo's signature din of roaring babel), occasionally all the readers will coalesce into a short-lived synchronization, having randomly fallen upon a passage common to all the iterations, so that for a brief time, everyone is declaiming the same lines in unison, reading exactly the same thing in perfect choral uniformity. But this concurrence will only hold for a moment or two, and then the voices wobble out of sync, reverting back to their default state of dissonant polyphony (punctuated every now and then by the sounds of depraved violence that surge in from the piazza whenever the front door is opened, like the looped soundtrack of an old video game).

When observing the patrons who congregate at the Bar Pulpo on any given Thursday "nite" (some of whom are actual fathers and daughters and some of whom are role-playing fathers and daughters) and whose ranks the authors of this volume have joined, it's exceedingly difficult to differentiate conversation from folktale, because their seemingly extemporaneous exchanges are frequently also verbatim recitations from the spoken-word karaoke screens.

We often have the eerie feeling, as we traverse the text, that the Chalazians themselves (among the most literate peoples on earth) are reading aloud along with us. Or, put another way, there's a mirroring reciprocity at play here: we're reading what the characters are reading and the characters are reading what we're reading.

Then there's this whole, weird little interlude with the "lozenge"—

PATIENT

Just as readers on both sides of the proscenium reflect one another, the Divine Hermit and the Chalazian Mafia Faction warlord, also consubstantial, surprise each other in the men's room mirror. Madness, Criminality, *Devequt* (cleaving to the divine), and Abstruse Mathematics constitute the four pillars of the Kermunkachunkian *Weltanschauung*—

OPTOMETRIST

I'm sorry, the *what*?

PATIENT

The Kermunkachunkian *Weltanschauung*...

She coughs, clears her throat.

The OPTOMETRIST *reaches into a jar on his desk and fishes out a lozenge of some sort.*

OPTOMETRIST

Would you like one?

PATIENT

Thank you.

She unwraps the lozenge, puts it in her mouth, and resumes reading—

PATIENT

Madness, Criminality, *Devequt* (cleaving to the divine), and Abstruse Mathematics constitute the four pillars of the Kermunkachunkian *Weltanschauung*—

OPTOMETRIST

Has anyone ever told you that you look like a young version of [inaudible]?

It's an intriguing remark, given the fact that, since she hasn't come out from behind the phoropter, we've never seen her face.

PATIENT

(shrugs, sucking on the lozenge)

I get Vanessa Hudgens now and then.

OPTOMETRIST

(tilts his head, scrutinizes her for a moment)

Yeah, I can see that. Alright—

(he checks the lenses on the phoropter)

Why don't we just pick up where we left off?

PATIENT

Madness, Criminality, *Devequt* (cleaving to the divine), and Abstruse Mathematics constitute the four pillars of the Kermunkachunkian *Weltanschauung*—

The OPTOMETRIST's *cellphone buzzes on the desk. He checks the caller ID.*

OPTOMETRIST

I'm sorry. I have to take this—

He turns away from the PATIENT *and speaks in furtive Yiddish, cupping his free hand over his mouth to muffle the sound even further. The conversation takes about a minute and a half, after which he places the phone back down on the desk.*

PATIENT

*(she says this as she peers through the phoropter,
so it appears as if she's still reading from
the Snellen chart projected on the opposite wall)*

A gentle, dignified man in his mid-sixties with a good-natured, ready smile, crow's feet accentuating the glint in his eyes, the Optometrist has lived a harrowing life. Both his parents were killed in a horrific home invasion (they were the invaders, *not* the occupants). Only five years old at the time, he was sent to live with a group of optometrists in Death Valley. He returned to the East Coast as a young, idealistic practitioner. After losing everything during the Night of the Broken Glasses, when neo-Nazis targeted Jewish optometrists, smashing all their lenses and frames, he refused to allow rancor to detract from the conscientious care of his patients (many of whom were themselves neo-Nazis). He methodically rebuilt his practice and, in 2023, was voted "New Jersey's Most Optimistic Optometrist." In his spare time (evenings and weekends), he's involved with a group of optometrists from all over the country who are working to provide MS-13 with nuclear weapons.

Though not without some basis in fact, this is probably just an astigmatic misreading of the chart, an instance of what optometrists call the "Ouija Board Effect (an unconscious permutation of the letters), or, most likely, just the lozenge talking.

OPTOMETRIST

*(as in a reality show "confessional" in which
a cast member talks directly to the camera)*

When we're not—

(whispers, with a wink)

—smuggling centrifuge components...we like to say—

(he points to the Snellen chart)

N'est-ce pas beau comme la littérature? Isn't it lovely as literature?

When the OPTOMETRIST *says "we," he means "We, the descendants of Spinoza, the Lens Grinder."*

OPTOMETRIST

(returning to the PATIENT)

How's this? Any better? Sharper?

By this point, only a melting sliver of lozenge remains in the PATIENT's *mouth.*

PATIENT

Sharper.

Many of the Divine Hermits who were willing to sit down for interviews used the exact same words to describe their mothers: "hard-drinking, chain-smoking, prone to writing wildly salacious emails, hitting Reply All, and coyly feigning embarrassment—'Ooops!'"

But Chalazians are unreconstructed animists, ascribing subjectivity and agency to almost all inanimate objects. They have sophisticated protocols that enable them to talk to and learn from their hair pomade, their cigarettes, their weapons, etc. These experiences are grounded in a cultural context that is markedly different from ours, so readers of *Last Orgy of the Divine Hermit* may initially be reluctant to view a wad of toilet paper, a wall-mounted soap dispenser, or an automatic hand dryer as a "teacher" or a "guru," but this is a fundamental concept, if not the sine qua non, of their metaphysical system.

And although the piazza is known as "the bullring of the nondiscursive real"—the place where "the real shit goes down"—the men's room at the Bar Pulpo is also a "bullring of the nondiscursive real." (And it is obviously the place where the *real shit* really does go down.)

The violence on the piazza seems indecipherable to the layperson (especially when viewed through the muck-encrusted windows of the Bar Pulpo), but to the Divine Hermits, the savage interplay of the sub-factions has all the legibility and inexorable logic of the lettered tiles they shuffle so purposefully at the Floating Casino on Lake Little Lake.

Once a young man or a young woman makes the decision to leave the Chalazian Children's Theater for the Chalazian Mafia Faction and "enter the piazza"—dousing themselves in the colognes that distinguish their sub-factions—their life expectancies shrink to a matter of several months.

It is out on the piazza that they "act out." Here we behold another universe of discourse in which quasi-suicidal, indiscriminate carnage is seen as the articulation of a certain Anthropocene *élan*. Doomstruck, the hero rushes to his death as a young husband rushes to his bride on their wedding night.

When a Chalazian woman says about a guy that he "cleans up good," she means bathed in his own blood.

In late medieval chivalric romances, Chalazian Mafia Faction street soldiers were frequently portrayed as miniaturized mechanomorphic vermin, scurrying behind the toilets in the men's rooms of bars.

In the winter, the temperatures plummet to absolute zero, and the piazza becomes a two-dimensional space, like the reproduction of a Breughel painting. And the tiny, almost subatomic, CMF mechanomorphic vermin—like those lettered tiles—exist in a state of blurry flux, capable of occupying an infinite number of locations simultaneously.

OPTOMETRIST

Beautiful. Now…how about this? Can you make out anything?

PATIENT

That's a tiny font, bro!

OPTOMETRIST

I know. Do the best you can.

PATIENT

I'm guessing here…

Faux discotheque ceviche…Funicular sugar tub…time machine?

The OPTOMETRIST *exchanges lenses in the phoropter.*

OPTOMETRIST

How's that? Can you make out anything now?

PATIENT

Full disclosure: the author and his marvelous daughter, Gaby, visited me at my office at Texas State Tech College in Waco, with the ostensible purpose of soliciting an introduction to their ethnography, *Last Orgy of the Divine Hermit*. This was not a complete surprise given the fact that I am one of the few academics who's actually been to Chalazia, although I focused my research exclusively on the Chalazian Children's Theater and deliberately did not extend my fieldwork to the Chalazian Mafia Faction, having deemed that—and I admit this unabashedly—*far* too dangerous an undertaking. Kermunkachunk is the most insanely violent city on the face of the earth, so you really do have to salute the two of them for their courage. I say this somewhat grudgingly, because the author—whose name I will not mention—is a vile human being, a disgusting, pathetic alcoholic. His daughter, Gaby, on the other hand, is just fantastic, a charming, poised, brilliant young woman. *Very* attractive. Gorgeous. Super-hot, actually.

PATIENT

Until he introduced her, I had no idea that was his daughter. I'd assumed they were a "couple" of some sort. I thought she was an escort, frankly—the age disparity, the shocking disparity in their appearances and deportment. Gaby is breathtaking, beguiling, poised. The author, on the other hand, is a small, scrofulous man, an alcoholic, the sclera of his eyeballs a jaundiced yellow. Her buoyant aplomb is always in stark contrast to his excruciating sense of inadequacy. They are so utterly dissimilar in every conceivable way as to throw into serious doubt the possibility of any consanguinity. But father and daughter they are.

This was an hour-long visit in the course of which he vomited on himself and urinated through his trousers. And he was wearing these leg warmers like he was fucking Bob Fosse or something.

He was like this filthy little drunken midget in leg warmers.

And although we're avoiding the mention of his name so as not to encourage copycats, his last book, *Gone with the Mind*, has sold barely two thousand copies since it was published in 2016. To put that in some perspective, *Love Italian Style: The Secrets of My Hot and Happy Marriage* by Melissa Gorga from *The Real Housewives of New Jersey* has sold close to fifteen thousand copies. While we're at it, *Turning the Tables: From Housewife to Inmate and Back Again* by Teresa Giudice (from the same show) sold ten thousand hardcover copies and twenty thousand e-books the first week it was out.

You'd think his also being from New Jersey might have boosted his sales a bit, but it obviously didn't help.

Nor does it help matters that he stinks. (Seriously, if your idea of a prepossessing individual is a sixty-five-year-old, reeking, incontinent little fop—he wears a huge pair of Pepto Bismol–pink Beats headphones around his neck like a sort of cravat—this is your guy.)

He'd be sitting there, slumped on the couch, eyes half shut, nodding off, head lolling, and suddenly he'd try to stand up and he'd promptly fall down, and there he'd remain on the floor for some time, balled up like an armadillo. I mean, this is what we're dealing with here.

Half staggering, half crawling, he looks like he's dying. Of something—cirrhosis, hepatic encephalopathy, Fournier's gangrene, Creutzfeldt-Jakob, perhaps, I don't know. (I'm a social scientist at a state university and unfortunately have neither the medical training nor the necessary instrumentation to render a diagnosis with any degree of certainty.) But I clearly remember thinking to myself, This guy isn't gonna make it through the year. Here was a man in a state of premature putrefaction, a man already colonized by necrophagic insects.

His daughter, on the other hand, his daughter…oh my god! She is *very* much alive! She's spectacular! Very beautiful, sophisticated, soigné. She's a filmmaker, very glamorous.

He alternately called her "Gaby," "Higgsly," "Minnie Mizuhō," "Mitzie," "Yanny"—at first, I thought, her given name and the usual complement of affectionate nicknames. But in hindsight, I've become convinced that he was thoroughly bewildered, in his demented drunkenness, as to who this person actually was.

Was this Gaby, was it Higgsly, was it Minnie Mizuhō, was it Mitzie or Yanny? I really think at times he had no idea.

The afternoon was an unending succession of cringe-inducing episodes.

I have a reproduction of Tullio Crali's painting *Nose Dive on the City* in my office. The idiot kissed it. He'd brought along his robotic service dog and it took an enormous dump in the middle of the floor. There was a bar code on the turd, which smelled like pumpkin spice, and which he then inserted— with excruciating difficulty because he was so drunk—up into his own ass.

All this would have been merely sad and pathetic were there not this nauseating whiff of self-satisfaction about him.

There seems to be a pus-filled doughnut at the core of his very being. (I knew another guy like this in high school. He was born with a pilonidal cyst instead of a heart. But he went on to become a wildly successful musician. We knew him back then in Bellmead, Texas, as little Danny Gonzáles; the world came to know him as Elton John. The rambunctious rock star leapt to the top of the national organ transplant list and received the heart of a young Dutchman who'd died in a motocross acci- dent; Elton's pilonidal cyst was given to a boy in Israel who was born without one and from whom the five-time Grammy winner still receives a Hanukkah card each and every year—

OPTOMETRIST

OK, hold on one sec...

He fiddles with the lenses in the phoropter.

OPTOMETRIST

Try now.

PATIENT

There seems to be a pus-filled doughnut at the core of his very being. His "act," this performative morbidity, is intended, I believe, as a kind of gag or stunt which he thinks will somehow amuse us, somehow win us over, such is his deteriorating mentality: he walks in circles, his default expression (his "resting face") is the simpering, blinking look of a hapless animal in the jaws of its predator, about to be yanked under.

More than anything else, though—the stench of him!

But it was all worth it. Because of Gaby.

There's a marvelous (and still shocking) scene in the 1947 film *Cynthia* (starring Elizabeth Taylor) in which the meek, chronically ill, overprotected teen, having experienced a flourishing resurgence, a libidinal awakening (she's fallen in love with a classmate), achieves a sort of Bataillean epiphany of abjection, dragging her prom dress through the mud in a kind of Dionysian conga line, singing her high school fight song.

Gaby is so much like the young Elizabeth Taylor in that film. That grave charm. Elegant, demure, reticent. The saintliness of an invalid. The chaste hauteur of a medieval ascetic like Teresa of Ávila or Catherine of Siena. But inside are all the coiled springs of life! All that primal, erotic life force churning underneath!

In 1946, during an idle period between *National Velvet* and *Courage of Lassie,* Taylor wrote a short, depraved book about

49

her pet chipmunk entitled *Nibbles and Me*. No less a figure than Henry James commented:

> If Joan Rivers had gone to the electric chair instead of Ethel Rosenberg, this is the book she would have written. Compulsively readable. I binged all fourteen volumes sitting under the dryer at the Kim Seung Hee Hair Salon in Palisades Park, New Jersey.

The PATIENT *peeks out from behind the phoropter just long enough to shoot a knowing grimace at the* OPTOMETRIST *concerning the dubious chronology suggested here (James died in 1916), and then reassumes her position behind the machine.*

The smoke from the OPTOMETRIST*'s cigar forms the spectral figure of James (in tweed three-piece suit, high-stiff-collared shirt, and wide ascot tie), which floats next to the Snellen chart like a Javanese shadow puppet. Now it's rotating fast, spinning... lip-syncing the lyrics from Robyn's "Dancing on My Own":*

"I'm right over here / Why can't you see me?"

OPTOMETRIST

Do you see that?!

Playacting, he says this with a sort of breathless amazement, even though this is a standard part of the optometric exam, designed to test for depth perception problems, the optokinetic nystagmus reflex, amblyopia, etc.

PATIENT

It looks like the black silhouette of soft serve on a cone, like a Dairy Queen, but the negative image of it.

He switches lenses in the phoropter.

OPTOMETRIST

How about now?

PATIENT

About the same.

OPTOMETRIST

(making a few notations)

That's OK. Let's pick up where we left off.

PATIENT

In 1946, during an idle period between *National Velvet* and *Courage of Lassie*, Taylor wrote a short, depraved book about her pet chipmunk entitled *Nibbles and Me*. No less a figure than Henry James commented:

> If Joan Rivers had gone to the electric chair instead of Ethel Rosenberg, this is the book she would have written. Compulsively readable. I binged all fourteen volumes sitting under the dryer at the Kim Seung Hee Hair Salon in Palisades Park, New Jersey.

Though frequently taught together with Ulysses S. Grant's *Memoirs*, it's hard to imagine two books the circumstances of whose composition were more dissimilar: the pampered, bucolic environment in which, presumably, Taylor wrote *Nibbles and Me* and the grim travails that attended the composition of Grant's *Memoirs* (in perilous financial straits and determined to provide his wife with a suitable amount of money to live on, Grant struggled to complete the volume despite the agony he was in from the throat cancer that would kill him only a few days after he finished).

One imagines the two of them scribbling away in adjoining cubicles. What a movie that would have made! The dying general and the starlet. Ernst Lubitsch comes to mind!

Gaby said something that afternoon—a comparison of Lubitsch and John Hughes, I think—that was so smart, so dazzlingly smart, that I can't even remember what it was. I just remember the physical sensations, that sharp intake of breath, the commotion deep in one's bowels, that one experiences in the presence of someone *that* brilliant, *that* erudite.

"I believe in the vision, you don't!" he snarled at me at one point, with what seemed like genuine vehemence, but apropos of what exactly I'd be hard put to say. Was he referring to his methodological approach as an ethnographer or perhaps to the Chalazian Mafia Faction's ideology of violently opposing everyone and everything, their belief in being in a state of trance and perpetual war? (There are CMF street soldiers, some fresh out of the Chalazian Children's Theater, who are able to MacGyver fully functional .45-caliber semiautomatic "ghost guns" entirely out of yarn and snow globes.) Or was it something else entirely, perhaps something literally about vision?

The PATIENT *pauses*—

PATIENT

Vision... That's amazing, isn't it?

OPTOMETRIST

(suddenly the "cool dad")

Awesome. It's next-level.

But this was a man who'd been targeted by the neo-Sturmabteilung trolls, who'd survived their Twitter pogroms, who, despite his stooped frailty and Parkinsonian tremors, was a man of steel who reveled in combat, a Jekyll and Hyde, actually, whose soul at night trawled heaven's demimonde, a serial killer of angels . . . an optometrist.

OPTOMETRIST

But we need to forge ahead. Whatever the cost. We neither forgive nor forget.

PATIENT

There are CMF street soldiers, some fresh out of the Chalazian Children's Theater, who are able to MacGyver fully functional .45-caliber semiautomatic "ghost guns" entirely out of yarn and snow globes. Or was it something else entirely, perhaps something literally about vision?

The author liked to whisper in my ear. He'd grab me by my shirtsleeve and pull me down to his level. (He had a powerful grip, like a little chimp on PCP.)

He confided to me, sotto voce (concerned, I assumed, that Gaby was not in the right "headspace" to hear this information), that he suffers from PTSD and dissociative identity disorder, and that he self-medicates with alcohol.

"Seriously?" I asked.

And he waved the question away.

He had this very effeminate way of waving his hand in the air, as if to disperse a bad smell (his own, presumably), whenever you broached something that vexed or embarrassed him.

"N'en parlons plus," he'd say. "Let's forget it!"

Sometimes he talked as if he and his daughter were about to embark upon their very first working sojourn in Kermunka-chunk, and sometimes he made it sound as if they'd just returned from their final trip.

I guess I should have asked Gaby. But, honestly, she makes me forget what I want to say.

Gaby's *unreal.* She's like some CRISPR baby who's blossomed into the most exquisite, refined, intellectually audacious young woman who ever existed. I'm serious!

But he—oh my fucking god!—he's super-annoying. He is easily the most tedious man on the fac⸱ ⸳f the earth (a title which all the drunks I've ever known assiduously covet), repeating the same things over and over and over again. Every five minutes, he'd look at the rubber band I had wrapped around my finger and ask me if it was an authentic Waffen-SS *Totenkopfring* (death's head ring).

> "My dead puggle, who is my guru and my Butoh teacher,
> came to me in a dream last night
> and gave me a new name:
> 'Fizzy Physiognomy.'"

He must have repeated that a dozen times in the hour he was here.

And there *is* something blurry, something indistinct, about the author (the "father," we might as well call him at this point).

But whereas he seems enshrouded in a swarm of flies, Gaby radiates an immaculate, luminous, shimmering aura, and it was my distinct impression, that afternoon in my book-cluttered office in Waco, that she is one of those rare individuals who can "dialectically experience reality in the process of uninterrupted becoming" *and* be super-super-hot (the latter, of course, an effect of the former).

Have I mentioned recently that he repeats the same things over and over and over again? He said (multiple times) that he was wearing a mask and special iris-reconfiguring contact lenses to foil facial recognition and biometric ID systems. (All I saw were the bloodshot eyes and sallow, blotchy face of a career alcoholic.) He said that the ghost of his dead puggle dictated *Last Orgy of the Divine Hermit* to a court stenographer, which is why it's in the form of an interrogatory or deposition.

Late in the book, in one of his drunken soliloquies at the Bar Pulpo (presumably read from one of the spoken-word karaoke screens), he contends that he and his daughter don't even conduct their own ethnographic fieldwork, that the ghost of the dead puggle commands *Heinzelmännchen*, or "little gnomes" (sometimes referred to, in variant iterations of the folktale, as "cunning little naked men"), to do their ethnographic research for them as he and his daughter "sleep" (i.e., drink).

As appealingly whimsical as this notion might be that gnomes do our work for us as we knock back shots at some bar, the author's identification with homunculi and the tiny robotic vermin and miniaturized mechanomorphic CMF street soldiers that scurry behind the toilets in the men's room at the Bar Pulpo is most likely an attempt to neutralize that very thing about which he feels the most abject, debilitating shame: his smallness. He has the little body of a sullen adolescent. By which I mean that tendency to rouse himself from his alcoholic torpor with a series of myoclonic spasms and— did I mention this before?—endlessly repeat himself like that fucking little leprechaun on PCP in the Lucky Charms commercial.

And he seems, in his sad, childish solipsism and insularity, to have developed an imaginary coterie of friends comprised exclusively of his own body parts. Interrupting an intense conversation Gaby and I were having about the Soviet film-maker Dziga Vertov, he suddenly announced, "My shoulders have completely different personalities from each other.

"This shoulder, Mike, is very bold. It would eat cat poop and make speeches from a balcony if it could! Very meth & alligators. This other one, Ike, is quiet, very introverted, very insular. For Ike, life is an elliptical fever dream, very goth, very Emily Dickinson.

"Have you ever heard anyone go on the way I do?! Have you ever heard anyone anthropomorphize his scapular asymmetry the way I do?" he asked, basking in the spotlight, the belle of the ball.

But he gave me a murderous look, his upper lip raised to expose his incisors.

He knew I loved his daughter.

He knew before any of us.

* * *

At times I felt terribly embarrassed on Gaby's behalf. (During these inane soliloquies, she'd listen and smoke her cigarette and nod in assent.) It was obvious she'd intended this to be an amiable and productive meeting of colleagues who shared a common field of study (Chalazia).

There's a marvelous German word for that, for that feeling of vicarious embarrassment...fuck...what's that word?...uh... fuck!...uh...uh...fuck...*Fremdschämen!*

I felt this overwhelming sense of, one might say, *Fremdschämen* when her father would...well, you can fill in the blank at this point. (His scapular asymmetry was due to dominant use of one limb, of his writing hand. Writing...ha! He printed like a child.)

The PATIENT *stops, squints—*

PATIENT

Is that right? "There's a marvelous German word for that, for that feeling of vicarious embarrassment...fuck...what's that word?... uh...fuck!...uh...uh...fuck...*Fremdschämen!* I felt this overwhelming sense of, one might say, *Fremdschämen* when her father would...well, you can fill in the blank at this point. (His scapular asymmetry was due to dominant use of one limb, of his writing hand. Writing...ha! He printed like a child)"?

OPTOMETRIST

Yes. That's perfect.

PATIENT

That's right? "Uh…fuck!…uh…uh…fuck…*Fremdschämen!*"

OPTOMETRIST

Close enough.

PATIENT

But Gaby, who, in her loving, filial impulse to protect him, to elevate him, and to restore a sense of cordial dignity to the proceedings, would invariably come to the rescue with something completely witty and charming, finally says (salvaging an afternoon which, at that point, seemed almost irretrievably lost), "Gentlemen, we're entering the realm of cephalopod neurophysiology here, of individual tentacles innervated to the extent that they literally have minds of their own. But once you grant a certain degree of subjectivity, of *agency* to your joints and your limbs and extremities, it can prompt all sorts of disconcerting insecurities."

She took a deep drag on her cigarette, its tip sizzling red, and then exhaled…

"I've begun to wonder," she said, frowning, but with a wink for her dad's benefit, "if my left hand even likes me anymore or if, at this point, it's just sticking around for the manicures."

She was referring to the hand that held her cigarette, which inscribed little whorls of smoke in the air as she spoke and gesticulated…which drew my attention to her fingernails, each of which bore a tiny, perfect, shiny reproduction of Seurat's *A Sunday Afternoon on the Island of La Grande Jatte*. (We'll take up the issue of whether paintings lose their Benjaminian "aura" when transferred to fingernails on next week's podcast, when our guest will be Lexi Martone, the nail artist featured in the new TLC reality series *Unpolished*.

I will also be conducting a Graduate Seminar Luncheon entitled "How a Hydrocephalic Garden Gnome and His Astonishing Daughter Wrote the Definitive Ethnographic Study of the Chalazian Mafia Faction." This will take place on Thursday, April 23, 12 to 2 p.m. at the Jack in the Box at 1525 Interstate 35 North in Waco.)

They were such a *mésalliance,* these two (if one can apply that term to a father so clearly outclassed by his own daughter). I do love her. No use denying it any longer.

Also, she has a lovely singing voice (more about which later).

Had so much fun at the NJ Society of Optometric Physicians party last night! (I never knew there was a bowling alley in the Port Authority!) Sorry I'm so terrible. Damn arthritis. Great seeing you and Irv and Phil. By the way, I fell in love too on the bus back home. A big, blowzy, lumpen woman, peroxide blonde hair with black roots, puffy coat opened to a see-through white tank top...

I'm an old man. I can't do this work forever. At this point, my arthritis is making it difficult for me to get the lenses in and out of the phoropter. It would be wonderful to retire and to have a woman like that as a companion, as a comrade...

I was sending invitations to her in this monotonic, almost liturgical telepathic voice. In Latin: Sit on this old optometrist's face. Asphyxiate me. Cannibalize me. (Wasn't it Elias Canetti who said "The earth asphyxiated by the letters of the alphabet"?)

I want you to walk around Costco with my enucleated eyeballs in your bra.

These fourteen words festooned conspicuously across the blank page, in the middle of the Snellen chart, in the middle of the spoken-word karaoke screen, crayoned in big characters in the middle of a poster out on the piazza...

I WANT YOU TO WALK AROUND COSTCO WITH MY ENUCLEATED EYEBALLS IN YOUR BRA.

Shaking his head with laughter, the kind old OPTOMETRIST *approaches and checks the* PATIENT'*s eyes with a handheld retinoscope. Then he switches lenses in the phoropter, etc.*

OPTOMETRIST

How about this? Can you make out any of it now?

PATIENT

Oh my god! I wasn't even close!

OPTOMETRIST

That's OK. Can you read it for me now?

PATIENT

I've known other men like this — small, smelly, childish, bro-ken, unscrupulous, alcoholic men. They almost inevitably have brilliant, beautiful daughters. It's a fairly standard folk-loric motif. I'm from central Texas, though. I'm accustomed to stoic men, to men who — whatever the vagaries of life, whatever the reversals of fortune that life's thrown at them — preserve their equanimity (my father was a mortician, and he maintained the same imperturbable sangfroid I saw on the faces of his cadavers), unlike this dude who weeps uncontrol-lably at the mere mention of his dead puggle, Lilli. I have a feeling, though, that this particular small, smelly, childish, broken, unscrupulous, alcoholic man thinks his particular shtick is "special." (Well, it's not.)

But G's shtick *is* special and it rocks my world.

And the small, smelly, childish, broken, unscrupulous, alcoholic man and his brilliant, self-possessed, gorgeous daughter have written an extraordinary book.

There was something about this malignant narcissist (and probably closeted homosexual) who pomaded his hair with petroleum jelly and the splendid Gaby (perhaps his high-pitched cackle and her unflagging solicitude) that evoked, *mutatis mutandis* and however imperfectly, the mad scientist/beautiful daughter trope that circulated in so many of the movies I used to see with my own drunken dad at that old, dilapidated drive-in theater in Anarene: in René Clair's *Paris Qui Dort,* with its crazed inventor, benevolent niece, and an immobilizing ray that paralyzes an entire city; in *Forbidden Planet,* with its reclusive philologist, Dr. Edward Morbius, and his miniskirted teenage daughter, Altaira (played by Anne Francis, who later starred in the television series *Honey West* as a voluptuous private investigator with a mole to the right of her lower lip and a pet ocelot); and in the incomparable *Eyes Without a Face,* with its deranged Dr. Génessier and his daughter, Christiane, whose face was horribly disfigured in an automobile accident for which Génessier was responsible.

Did I mention that he repeats himself over and over and over again? That he pulled me down to whisper in my ear that he uses alcohol to self-medicate for PTSD and dissociative identity disorder, disorders that he at first blamed on a botched first haircut by a barber who'd been gassed in World War I (a mustard gas attack at Ypres)?

Then he thought this over, his contemplative posture a cataleptic rigidity, accompanied by the buzz of flies attracted to his necrotic body odor, by the whistle of escaping gases, the cadaverine and putrescine, the hydrogen sulfide, the methanethiol and dimethyl disulfide. As I mentioned before, my dad was an undertaker. I grew up with the smells of decomposing bodies.

"Nah, nah, maybe it wasn't that," he said, waving at the air with his hand.

He floated an alternate theory. For his first haircut, his parents had taken him to the barbershop inside the Park Sheraton Hotel on Fifty-Sixth Street and Seventh Avenue, where he was seated in the chair next to Albert Anastasia when the Gambino boss and Murder Inc. hit man was assassinated. (After the first fusillade, Anastasia tried to attack his killers, but in a moment of panic and confusion, the bullet-riddled mobster had actually lunged at the gunmen's reflection in the wall mirror of the barbershop.) He said it was horrible, that Anastasia had been "like a father to me." (Which was total bullshit, by the way.)

Then he said, "Nah, nah..."

And he suggested that maybe *this* was the traumatic event that caused his PTSD and dissociative identity disorder:

Choking on an Atomic Fireball
after seeing his grandma's bush in a beach cabana.

"If you can guess the right answer, you can have my daughter's hand in marriage," said the drunk little father.

As I thought it over, Gaby smoked, a wry smile on her face.

Finally, I hazarded a guess: "Choking on an Atomic Fireball after seeing your grandma's bush in a beach cabana..."

"Nope," he said.

"Anyway, I have a boyfriend," Gaby said. "His name is Ichiro Matsumoto. He's a scientist. Half his face was horribly disfigured in a radiation accident. Half is perfectly normal."

I was certain (I still am) that I'd guessed correctly.

It all seemed like a routine they'd performed before, like some sort of a con game out of *Paper Moon*. (Again, to what end, I'd be hard-pressed to say.)

He told me his nom de guerre when he wrestled professionally was "Tater Tot Poutine."

More bullshit.

He said his best friend in junior high school was MMA lightweight champion Khabib Nurmagomedov.

"So you went to junior high in Makhachkala, Dagestan?" I asked.

"Yeah..." he said. "But I transferred because they didn't have a good writing program."

And more bullshit.

I asked him what accomplishment in his life he was proudest of.

He said passing out drunk next to a passed-out-drunk Billy Idol on a couch at Danceteria in 1983.

Seventeen years earlier, in 1966, *Honey West* was canceled after just one season, and Anne Francis's mole, hit by an errant blast of gamma radiation, reproduced itself a trillion times over and fell from the sky in great swirling storms, a blizzard of moles, pitting windshields and accumulating in drifts several feet high on the ground. This constituted a mytho-historical, *ectopic* event, i.e., an actual event that never happens. Or perhaps a *herniated* event, a contemporaneous event that bulges through the space-time membrane and presents as chronologically anterior to when it actually occurred—in this case, a 1966 event that herniated, protruding into the Precambrian eon.

And for several days after, the Children of the Steppe (now extinct) cavorted in the high drifts of black moles. Those vacant-eyed, feral creatures (who shared the Steppe at that time with, uh…with CGI mollusks and tardigrades) would no longer experience life as a continuous flow, but as stop-motion, acceleration, deceleration, reverse action, split frame, pixilation, as spasmodic oscillations between paralysis and vivification.

Until finally these "children" (traditionally depicted in Chalazian folklore with fangs, with tapeworms wriggling out from their eye sockets), now sufficiently deranged by the ergot fungi in the moles, would leap at one another and rip themselves into a thousand shreds.

How then did the Chalazian Steppe (whose aboriginal population, until very recently, lived in inflatable ball pits and bounce houses) turn white, a reflective, mirrorlike white? It constitutes, after all, one of *LOOTDH*'s three talismanic mirrors: the mirror in the men's room at the Bar Pulpo, the reflecting surface of Lake Little Lake, and the specular crust of the Steppe itself (each of which transfigures by confounding surface and depth, generating at each moment that "crisis of belief" that is so distinctly Chalazian, so *totally* Chalazian).

There have been two standard explanations:

- White rust formed when zinc in the moles was exposed to hydrogen and oxygen in the atmosphere, creating zinc hydroxide.
- The moles were chocolate (this is now the prevailing theory) and underwent a process called "fat bloom" in which triglycerides in the cocoa butter migrate through the mole and crystallize, leaving a glaze-like layer on the surface.

These glazed moles…
This glazed Steppe.

The Steppe, in Chalazian folklore, is akin to the "place in France where the alligators dance"—that is, a vortex of Satanic Maoism with Kenneth Anger as its Leni Riefenstahl.

OPTOMETRIST

Perfect.

PATIENT

But mostly the father is sad—both in the sense of being desperately unhappy and of being pathetic, i.e., a sad spectacle.

Like someone who's never lived up to his early promise, he compulsively fidgets with his shoelaces, with the laces of his sneakers. He sits there tying and untying and retying, and tying and untying, trying to achieve a perfectly equivalent tightness between the right and the left, an impossible parity. Now this one's tighter. Now that one's tighter. This old, disgusting, ragged pair of sneakers.

Oh, how one suffered the virtuousness, the reproach of his impecunity! (And, of course, when Gaby went to the ladies' room, he asked me for money.)

True, these specific tropes of asymmetry (the shoulders, the laces, etc.) are not recapitulated in *LOOTDH*, with its infinite regress of fathers and daughters "all the way down," but one could certainly say that the asymmetry of the father/daughter dyad is its defining characteristic, its sine qua non, although, at some point, they—the father and the daughter—do converge, as it were, in reciprocal mimesis.

And weeks later, I'd find myself feeling considerably more charitable, more gently analytical, if you like, when I thought back to his behavior that afternoon.

The tying and untying—that rocking back and forth, almost a swaying in prayer. It's the sort of repetitive movement, the sort of restricted, circumscribed behavior one might associate with autism. The laces here, the laces there, the laces here, the laces there, over and over and over again. Back and forth and back and forth. From shoe to shoe. Akin to the swaying back and forth, the *shuckling* we might observe in readers of the Big-Character Posters out on the piazza.

Meanwhile, back at the OPTOMETRIST's office—

The PATIENT, *always behind that phoropter. That big lens machine that becomes her face essentially. Her "eyes without a face." Like someone/something staring out from one of Rodchenko's Constructivist advertising posters.*

PATIENT

Once I said, "It's unbearably hot in here. I apologize. The AC's not working. Maybe we should all strip down to our underwear. I do that sometimes when I'm grading papers."

They concurred, etc., etc.

She was fit and lithe.

His body was covered with the spider angiomas and Bier spots associated with serious liver disease.

It got very quiet. We could hear the gossiping sprites who lived in the water pipes.

The sun shone through the windows, projecting quadrilateral shapes of light on the walls.

The PATIENT *pauses, realizing that the Snellen chart she's reading from is a quadrilateral shape of light projected on the wall...*

We hear the whistling of the OPTOMETRIST *("Zip-a-Dee-Doo-Dah") as he switches lenses in the phoropter (a motific rhyme with the whistling of gases escaping from the dying, alcoholic father in Waco).*

Of course, there are no windows in this madman's laboratory. Is it day or night? What month, what year is it? One can't really know. A techno-utopian hyperspace, the OPTOMETRIST *and the* PATIENT *could survive here for thousands of years. It also recalls Plato's cave, whose projected shadows are replaced by the permutating letters of the Snellen chart.*

PATIENT

(continues reading)

LOOTDH is structured as a sublimated enticement to a fatalistic climax—the Last Orgy, the Dance of Death.

But it is in speaking of the Father and Daughter's one-hour sojourn in Waco, which was then considered the Riviera, the Deauville of central Texas, that the folklorists begin to go mad with rage and desire.

He had one very beautiful and lucid moment, one incongruously beautiful, touching moment when he suddenly lurched out of his catatonic stupor—during which I'd swear he had a bowel movement—and launched into a lovely, richly evoked reminiscence of Gaby as a little girl, of taking her one spring to Washington, DC, to see the cherry blossoms around the Tidal Basin, to the National Museum of Health and Medicine (which, at the time, was located within a wing of the Walter Reed Army Medical Center) to see the tumor that killed Ulysses S. Grant (a squamous cell carcinoma at the base of his tongue).

One time, the three of us were staring out the windows of my office. (The panes were almost too hot to touch. Such was the blinding central Texas sun.) Squinting, we saw someone carrying something. And then he was attacked by three other people. Like all the rest of us, from a distance, they'd confused these chemistry-class models of large molecules (polypeptides) with cake.

The PATIENT *pauses for a moment — she's been there.*

PATIENT

(continuing to read)

More than his tendency to vomit and urinate on himself and to weep at the slightest provocation (at the mention of his dead puggle, Lilli — a subject he himself continually broached — he'd tear at his clothes and pummel his own chest with his fists before collapsing in convulsive sobs), what I found most disturbing was his shameless propensity to name-drop, coyly insinuating personal, if not intimate, relationships with:

Sunny von Bülow
Mary Jo Buttafuoco
Famke Janssen
Oksana Baiul
Fin Tutuola
Lorena Bobbitt

Martha Stewart

Jeffrey Dahmer

Bobby Flay

Chef Boyar...

The PATIENT *is squinting.*

PATIENT

Chef Boyar...zee?

The OPTOMETRIST *switches lenses in the phoropter.*

PATIENT

Chef Boyardee.

OPTOMETRIST

Good.

PATIENT

One tolerates all his portentous, self-pitying valedictions—it's always this is the last *this* and the last *that,* "This is the last time my daughter and I will ever work together on an ethnography," "This is the last time I'll ever see you in Waco," "This is the *Last Orgy of the Divine Hermit,*" etc., etc.—in anticipation of something truly marvelous that Gaby might interject.

The French anthropologist Philippe Descola writes in *The Spears of Twilight* (*Les lances du crépuscule*), "Given that the common sense of some cultures is not the same as that of others, ethnologists must perforce sometimes make use of philosophers' instruments when they are out hunting in territory where the latter do not venture." And surely Gaby qualifies as a deft wielder of philosophers' instruments just as the Bar Pulpo and the piazza are territories where the latter do not venture.

Whereas the Father's contributions to the book itself— particularly easy to identify, given its theatrical format—tend to indulge in ponderous navel-gazing and a kind of witless scab-picking (at the end of the book, he requests an Uber and a UFO comes instead and takes him away—my immediate thought when I read that was, I hope the crew has a good supply of air freshener), Gaby's writing is of great subtlety and refinement. Her contributions (which are unmistakably, conspicuously "Gaby") are limpid, intricate, supple, silky, delicate, spontaneous, rapturously phrased. She manages both a breeziness, a *sprezzatura,* and a pungency. Whenever Gaby speaks, an uninhibited liveliness and charm is restored to the text. She saves the book. Hers is a happy, capering mind. A blithe skipping here, then there, then over there, but always looking back to make sure you're still with her, solicitous and kindhearted that way.

And I can't imagine that it's not Gaby—and Gaby alone—who was ultimately responsible for the book's remarkable scope and meticulous granularity. It's as if she combed through this sordid subculture in pursuit of its tiniest louse eggs in order to create this shimmering mosaic, this mandala of nits!

Gaby actually confided in me at some point that afternoon, perhaps during one of those interludes when her alcoholic father had passed out after hydroplaning on a slick of his own vomit, that because of the complexity of Kermunkachunk's criminal underground—there are said to be more sub-factions of the Chalazian Mafia Faction than there are atoms in the solar system—and the ever-proliferating indeterminacies in the Chalazian language (more about which later), their accumulated data was too voluminous to transmit over the internet, so it was placed on hard disks and flown back to the Wilhelm Klink Institute for Social Research in Bonn, Germany.

PATIENT

It's blurry now…uh…

hgsfcd lmgp ooeirv mxcn chvkuygbd nmoontp ydschgs dxwfasah sjdh nokpdkjbjv uyrbk fnmlkoihj yvfesd fwybgb nkpumppu rmewdfl

OPTOMETRIST

Can you read any of this or is it also too blurry?

PATIENT

No, I can read it—

At one point, with an alacrity and élan that characterize her generation's finest minds, she whipped out her phone and showed me a video of Russian weight lifter Tatiana Kashirina being administered smelling salts (ammonia inhalants) by her coach before her clean and jerk.

She also showed me a photo of a heavily tattooed L.A. Mexican gangbanger taking a bubble bath with a little extraterrestrial-looking monkey, adding, with a wink, "I like that lifestyle."

And although I wasn't at all sure what lifestyle she was referring to, I thought it was a super-charming, super-cute remark. It's just so *Gaby*—intimidatingly, castratingly erudite *and* super-cute, qualities never more manifest than when she and her father play Fuck Marry Kill at the Bar Pulpo sometime before he embarks on his Dance of Death.

(If you have the opportunity, try to see Gaby's *Mouchette on East 4th.* A shrewd and stylish feminist homage to Robert Bresson's 1967 film *Mouchette,* it culminates in its own sublime and emotionally devastating *Danse Macabre.*)

She also has a beautiful voice!

There's a scene in the book during which she sings Stephen Foster's "Hard Times Come Again No More" while her father chokes on his own saliva, and it's *amazing.*

There's a musicality to her very presence, to the modulating intonations in her speaking voice, to her gestures and movements which evoke classical Indian dance, a kinetic fluidity that conjures up images of multiarmed Hindu goddesses like Durga and Kali.

Sometimes I'd catch her just whistling to herself, like one of those insouciantly happy, chirping birds in *Snow White.* And it's not some inane, ditzy kind of whistling either. She's thinking about very abstruse Heideggerian sorts of things, like Heraclitus and Hölderlin, while she whistles, believe me.

This whistling is, of course, completely unlike the whistling gases of the moribund father (we might as well call him "Little Papi" at this point) or that of the OPTOMETRIST.

The PATIENT *suddenly stops, flushed with curiosity about how the Professor's Introduction could possibly include a reference to the* OPTOMETRIST. *Would the Professor somehow, intertextually, allude to her? she wonders, aquiver with mounting excitement. She wants him to.*

And you can sense her disappointment when the Professor returns to his animus toward the Father. There's a twinge of petulant impatience in her voice as she resumes her reading—

PATIENT

I try not to hate him.

He's not stupid. He's just a particularly unprepossessing person. A pathetic, disheveled, socially inept little man with a gigantic chip on his shoulder. A self-pitying lush who lurches unpredictably from belligerence to maudlin tears, who looks and smells like death warmed over.

But he's adept in his way; he has a certain armamentarium at his disposal, of which Gaby is, in a manner of speaking, an essential component.

I have dreams of literally shitting him. Of looking down into the toilet bowl and seeing that red face—mottled with broken blood vessels from a lifetime of alcohol abuse—seeing that floating red turd-face simpering up at me from the water.

There's also a dream in which I'm sitting by a gurney in the hallway of a clinic in the slums of some teeming megalopolis, and he looks up at me and asks, "How long do I have left, and how bad will it get?"

But I awake from this one hating him even more and spending the whole ensuing day seething, as I grade papers in my office, giving everyone Cs and Ds.

But Gaby…Gaby…Gaby.

I can't get her out of my mind.

I'm deeply in love with her. I know I am.

The PATIENT *pauses, sighs…*

PATIENT

(her eyeballs extruding little bubbly heart emojis as she reads)

Needless to say at this point, it's Gaby's book. Both in the sense of her stealing the show and in the sense of her— as is my strong suspicion—having done all the work. (I think he basically just throws things out there to see what your reaction will be, to see if he can get a rise out of you—which, I suppose, one could argue, constitutes a *kind* of "writing.")

Putting aside the criminal omission of Gaby as *coauthor* (she is, I suspect, the *sole author*), the book is a masterwork, a claim hardly to be seriously contested at this point in history. It is already considered the standard reference work on the Chalazian Mafia Faction.

No one has more cogently analyzed or more vividly portrayed the enigmatic figure of the Divine Hermit, whose frenzied saturnalias have the outward appearance of a man listlessly playing solitaire in his cell.

In the same way that Lichtenstein used Ben Day dots to denature and sublimate the gestural faktura of the expressionistic brushstroke, the Divine Hermits use letter permutation to denature and sublimate the violence of the Chalazian Mafia Faction, whose street soldiers slaughter their victims out on the piazza and enucleate them, flinging their eyeballs at the windows of the Bar Pulpo.

Notwithstanding my feelings about the father (who really is a revolting little scumbag, a weird little fucking drunken gnome—when he left, I drenched my hands in Purell!), and realizing that one makes this sort of judgment at one's peril, I think *Last Orgy of the Divine Hermit* may come to be read as one of the great anthropological adventures of modern literature. If I thought otherwise, I would never have agreed to write this Introduction.

On a more ominous note...

Several weeks after their visit, I received a dozen roses from the Father, the petals made out of prosciutto...which I took to be some sort of threat.

This was followed, several days later, by a vague invitation to join him and his daughter in Kermunkachunk ("at some point in the future"), an invitation I warily accepted. The letter was unsigned, but it was handwritten in his characteristically childish, block-lettered print. I say "childish" because it was so perfect, as if each letter were formed under the reproachful scrutiny of some bony, basilisk-breathed martinet standing over him.

He added as a postscript, referring presumably to *Last Orgy of the Divine Hermit*, the ethnography he and his daughter had yet to write:

> If Joan Rivers had gone to the electric chair
> instead of Ethel Rosenberg,
> this is the book she would have written.

OPTOMETRIST

OK, great. Now... can you read any of this?

PATIENT

Ryan Murphy's limited series about a nasal, anorexic, hand-cuffed Momofuku Noodle Bar dishwasher's festering toupee fetish—

OPTOMETRIST

Hold on for just a sec...

(he switches lenses in the phoropter)

How about now?

PATIENT

Oh wow!

OPTOMETRIST

From the top, if you don't mind—

PATIENT

Gerhard Richter's painting of a naked schizophrenic hunchbacked nurse (or nun, perhaps) feeding a toucan a fish stick was purchased by a Chalazian Mafia Faction godfather for his daughter's quinceañera for $4,500,000,000,000,000,000, 000,000,000,000,000,000,000,000,000,000,000,000,000, 000,000,000,000,000,000,000,000,000,000,000 and now hangs in the lobby of the Floating Casino.

OPTOMETRIST

Excellent.

PATIENT

There, nestled amidst the Bvlgari and Veuve Clicquot and Bottega Veneta showcases, it is flanked by two of Chalazia's most totemic works of art: a painting depicting the delirium of the piazza—hissing projectiles that generate waves of energy, hurtling trajectories of force propelled outward so that they impinge upon the viewer—and one of a crying clown seated on the toilet in one of the stalls of the men's room at the Bar Pulpo. Both appear to be crayon doodles that one might make on a place mat.

The Floating Casino (where Divine Hermits, levitating and ithyphallic, endlessly shuffle their lettered tiles) is a fabulous Qing dynasty villa that was purchased by a consortium of CMF warlords and transported from Hangzhou to Lake Little Lake (home to the world's only freshwater octopus) in 2035. Seen through the lake's mist, it seems to actually float in the air. The high-pitched drone of the speedboats, which continuously orbit this former *château de plaisance,* can be heard as far away as the piazza.

Focusing an ethnography (i.e., a folktale) on a drunk father and daughter who, before the father's Dance of Death, say goodbye to each other for the last time (the last orgy?) always risks a descent into sentimentality. But there's not even a smidgen of it here. Instead, we're treated to a grand exposition of the merciless ethos of the Chalazian Mafia Faction street soldier.

Just who (or what) are these dreaded, violent, unapproachable young people who once delighted audiences (of mostly relatives) at the Chalazian Children's Theater and now pelt the windows of the Bar Pulpo with the plucked eyeballs of their enemies?

In one scene, two men (police agents working undercover as Father and Daughter) walk into the Bar Pulpo, one wearing black jeans, a black velour V-neck, and desert boots, the other a knockoff Dolce & Gabbana teal miniskirt and matching bustier. They sit down at the bar, have a drink, reconnoiter the premises, and exit. Soon after they leave, a Chalazian Mafia Faction street soldier enters, casually huffing from a container of varnish remover and humming "All I Ask of You" from *Phantom of the Opera.* Even though we know he's just killed at least one of the cops—he's wearing his miniskirt and bustier and rolling his eyeballs in his hand like Captain Queeg—he still seems to us somehow charming, almost genteel, as he sits himself down at the bar and accepts a roofied drink from some perverted sex tourist. (The street soldier—whose exaggerated wink at the "audience" betrays a definite musical-theater background—put the Rohypnol in his *own* drink.) Despite the fact that it's one of the book's most delightful and richly evoked scenes, the budding friendship between this kid and the tourist—a beer-bellied American in a Midas cap—comes out of nowhere and feels dramaturgically unearned: a man strolls in from the piazza and serenades them, playing a lute made out of cardboard and dental floss...and then the street soldier disappears into the night, the cloud of ink into which he withdraws like an octopus.

How are Chalazian Mafia Faction street soldiers called to the piazza, to the wild scrambling and hurtling of bodies in that no-man's-land? We can hear them whetting the tines of their forks on the pavement stones, for god's sake!

Are they signaled somehow by the Divine Hermits, those levitating, ithyphallic, mystic zaddiqs, perpetually shuffling their lettered tiles at the Floating Casino? Or is this just something we want so much to be true? That the permutation of letters produces manifest reality.

One pockmarked young woman with the soulless eyes of a sociopath and a glue sniffer's rash around her mouth (who, only months ago, had delighted audiences in a Chalazian Children's Theater stage adaptation of *Amelia Bedelia*) says that, yes, they are signaled to come out to the piazza and that the signal feels like that tingling sensation in your nose just before you sneeze, the slightest twinge of sciatica at the top of the buttocks, a fizziness or a sizzling in the perineum—

The PATIENT *pauses, fishes out a tiny airline bottle of Tito's vodka from her bag, cracks it open, and takes a sip—the implication being, perhaps, that she's receiving "the signal."*

PATIENT

...a fizziness or a sizzling in the perineum.

OPTOMETRIST

Excellent.

PATIENT

These CMF street soldiers, whose weapons of choice are the Austrian-made Steyr M9 semiautomatic pistol and the melon baller, seek what the ancient Greeks called a *kalos thanatos*—a beautiful death. They seek their *aristeia*—their finest, and frequently final, scene—and even when attempting to justify their acts of gratuitous brutality, they typically resort to the lyrics of the songs they'd, up until recently, belted out onstage at the Chalazian Children's Theater. Responding to a question about how he can so casually gouge out the eyeballs of another human being, one gaunt young man, huffing Scotchgard as he speaks, says, "Who can explain it, who can tell you why? / Fools give you reasons, wise men never try," rotely regurgitating the lyrics of "Some Enchanted Evening" from Rodgers and Hammerstein's *South Pacific*.

As another glassy-eyed cadre slurs (a chemical odor on her breath from the butter-flavored no-stick cooking spray she continuously huffs): "The reality we perceive is a mere epiphenomenon arising from the underlying structure of the brain, which is itself an epiphenomenon arising from purely mathematical properties—topological homogeneity, supersymmetry, stochastic dynamics, etc., etc. In other words, reality is a surface effect of mathematics...which gets us back to the shuffling of the lettered tiles, the 'permutation of letters'...all the mystical shit that the Divine Hermits talk about all the time..."

Then, staring off into the distance, she murmurs something in Chalazian, something that sounds like (but most likely is not) "Justin Bobby...," as if she were beseeching Audrina Patridge's on-again, off-again boyfriend in the reality series *The Hills*, before convulsing and losing consciousness, as if it were just another day out on the piazza, as if suddenly, fleetingly, we were out on the moors of *Wuthering Heights*.

Later, reading from one of the Big-Character Posters mounted along the periphery of the piazza, she recites the poem whose final stanza has become the bloodcurdling *cri de guerre* of the Chalazian Mafia Faction:

> Sittin' on the dock of the bay
> (in Spider-Man pajamas),
> My wounded, trepanned skull swathed
> in a turban of bandages.
>
> No fucks to give.
> Raspberry beret.
> Transvaginal mesh.
>
> Neo-Nazi ménage à trois.
> Octopus neurophysiology.
> Illuminati intifada.
>
> Stay secret,
> Stay hydrated,
> Rock on.

According to *Last Orgy of the Divine Hermit,* the Chalazian Mafia Faction is riddled with *agents provocateurs,* and in many, if not all, sub-factions, *agents provocateurs* outnumber actual members. In fact, the most crucial prerequisite to becoming a member of the Chalazian Mafia Faction is that you are an *agent provocateur*—in other words, there are no members of the Chalazian Mafia Faction who are not *agents provocateurs.* Also, male CMF street soldiers prefer older women (and heavier women: a popular greeting used when encountering someone you haven't seen recently is "I liked you better fat").

To the young, male CMF street soldier, the haggard, world-weary look of a middle-aged woman slouched on a subway at the end of a workday, that exhausted, bedraggled, they-don't-pay-me-enough-for-this-shit, I-just-want-to-get-home, get-out-these-clothes, change-into-something-comfortable, microwave-a-bite-to-eat-and-watch-something-trashy-on-television look, is considered to be "super-hot." (In the book, a heavily armed stud swaggering across the piazza is shown a photo of the twenty-three-year-old *Sports Illustrated* swimsuit model Alexis Ren and makes a finger-in-the-mouth gagging gesture.)

For your average Kermunkachunkian street soldier, sex with a premenopausal woman is, if not completely taboo, considered weird.

These CMF thugs are taught that their martyrdom out on the piazza will lead to a paradise with a sort of chill, anodyne, Crate & Barrel vibe. Thanks to the recreational inhalation of nail polish remover, their brains turn to glass by the time most of them reach their mid-twenties, which few of them actually do. (The vitrified brain of a CMF street soldier, inlaid with jade and mother-of-pearl, is currently on display in the lobby of the Floating Casino on Lake Little Lake.)

So, *Last Orgy of the Divine Hermit* is not only a masterly examination of what it means to be a drunk father and daughter in a bar whose gore-encrusted windows are being perpetually pelted with the enucleated eyeballs of the victims of an internecine gang war, but also an unflinching examination of who we've become as passengers on a shipwrecked planet.

And, given the thousands of variants that stream across the spoken-word karaoke screens at the Bar Pulpo, it should come as no surprise that a recent version of the folktale casts the Father as an ethnographer and the Daughter as a glamorous filmmaker!

In another variant, the Daughter is neither beautiful nor sympathetic but an anti-Semitic, hatchet-faced spinster. In one of his final moments of lucidity, and literally grasping at straws (those poking out of his cans of Glucerna), the dying Father asks, "What do you think is going to happen to me?" The Daughter responds, "You're going to become something that's not you." And only then is the Father able to die peacefully, and the Daughter is magically transformed into a beautiful princess, a filmmaker.

Some versions don't even take place in Chalazia at all. In one, the Daughter has been accepted into the Columbia University graduate film studies program but can't decide whether she really wants to go or not. And instead of at the Bar Pulpo in Kermunkachunk, she meets the Father at Yakiniku Futago, a

Japanese barbecue restaurant (with a great bar) on 17th Street, between Fifth and Sixth Avenues in Manhattan, to discuss the matter.

In another version, the Father and Daughter (named Caesar and Little Madonna) are extinct, rodent-like mammals called *multituberculates* who've been kept in a cryostat for several years. They are finally reanimated by an elderly and eccentric paleontologist. In this one too, Little Madonna ultimately gets into the Columbia University graduate film studies program, etc., etc.

Over the course of the text, many other folktales are cited *en passant*—there's one about an inexhaustible stick of deodorant, another about a husband who loves his wife so much that he deliberately mistreats her at the end of his life so she'll be happy when he dies.

These are all the sorts of folktales (or "fact patterns," as they're called now) that flight attendants routinely pantomime in the aisle before takeoff.

There's a version in which one block of pure, condensed present is superimposed upon another block of pure, condensed present—a series of crystalline tableaux layered and compressed, layered and compressed into a single sepulchral moment.

And yet another, this one involving some American tourist in the Bar Pulpo who, exasperated when he can't elicit the location of the men's room from a non-English-speaking Chalazian waiter, exclaims, "Mind over matter doesn't matter if you're the Mad Hatter with a weak bladder who steals money from his friends and still has to sell all his soggy Depends on eBay anyway, esé!"

As in the poem by Pasolini ("A Desperate Vitality") that begins "As in a film by Godard," the book is in the form of a dialogue (with stage directions), an interview, perhaps one might even say a psychoanalytic session, but with the roles of analyst and analysand constantly shifting.

...then the Daughter's horribly disfigured Japanese scientist boyfriend arrives outside in his red Formula One Ferrari to pick her up, and here the book moves into its tonally richest register.

And yet, it's almost over before it starts.

Still, no one before has so sharply delineated the underlying architecture of the Chalazian *mentalité*—the savage psychopathology outside on the piazza, the serene gemütlichkeit inside the Bar Pulpo, the violent endopsychic turmoil in its sanctum sanctorum, its innermost realm: the men's room. No one before has so vividly theorized the sensation of being swallowed up into the serpent—the coiled Möbius strip—that is Chalazia, of being dragged down in its peristaltic undertow.

And the Snellen chart is a harbinger of the *ivresse du discours* at the book's end.

OPTOMETRIST

Great. Now...can you make out any of this?

PATIENT

Ummm...

Like Euripides's *The Bacchae* on the outside (with the bloody insanity out there on the piazza, the *sparagmos*) and Sophocles's *Oedipus at Colonus* on the inside (with the whole dying father/dutiful daughter trope going on), *Last Orgy of the Divine Hermit* distills a fantastic multiplicity of ethnographic minutiae, of straight-up, formfitting, en suite Chalazian Mafia shit, into a study of extraordinary theoretical density. It's like the offspring produced when some huge, encyclopedic disquisition is mated with a Chihuahua.

Don't be intimidated by its brevity!

OPTOMETRIST

Perfect.

PATIENT

One can't help but be struck by the exiguity of Chalazia. As someone says of the country—I'm assuming it was Gabs (with her inimitable panache)—"It's very finite."

There seem to be only four places in all of Kermunkachunk: Kermunkachunk International Airport, the Bar Pulpo, the piazza, and the Floating Casino on Lake Little Lake. Perhaps a fifth, the Ish-Delish Deli—but it's only alluded to; we never actually see it. (There's a production company, of course—Don't Let This Robot Suck Your Dick Productions—but again, we never see its offices, its facility.) And apparently, there's only one place in Greater Chalazia: the Steppe.

(Don't be intimidated by the brevity of the country!)

There's a similar exiguity of historical incident—that is to say, nothing has happened in Chalazia beyond the chocolate mole storms and the fat bloom, which precipitated the glazing of the Steppe; the fairly recent extinction of the Steppe's indigenous population (which had lived for millennia in inflatable bounce houses and ball pits); the chance encounter of a dying Ulysses S. Grant and a young Elizabeth Taylor; the proliferation of semiautomatic guns made of yarn and snow globes; Tatiana Kashirina's 193-kilo clean and jerk; the overrunning of Kermunkachunk by the Chalazian Mafia Faction on June 26, 2035; the mass suicide of the Divine Hermits (their flash mob Dance of Death); and the forced evacuation of the capital.

These are the only things that have *ever* happened. This is the tone row of Chalazian history. What at first appears mere scantiness is actually a system, a methodology. Chalazia is a twelve-tone country. Its folktales are twelve-tone folktales (endless permutations of a prescribed set of leitmotifs). And *Last Orgy of the Divine Hermit* is a twelve-tone ethnography, presenting itself as a kind of fractal homology to the country's dodecaphonic history and folklore. But *LOOTDH* goes much further. It suggests that *any* ethnography of *any* sort—whether it's an ethnography of Naxalite Maoists, Wall Street investment bankers, the Hmong refugees of Minneapolis, or Serbian football hooligans—must play these same twelve "notes," in inversion (denoted I), retrograde (R), or retrograde inversion (RI), in addition to its "original" or prime form (P):

1. The splintering of a children's theater
2. The tile shuffling ("letter permutation") of racketeering illuminati
3. Big-Character Posters and spoken-word karaoke screens
4. The rampant enucleation of eyeballs out on a piazza
5. A patient's astigmatic misreading of a Snellen chart
6. Mechanomorphic vermin that scurry behind the toilets in the men's room of a bar

7. A graduate seminar at a Jack in the Box in Waco
8. An Atomic Fireball in a beach cabana
9. The ascendency of a Dead Puggle
10. The arrival of a disfigured Japanese boyfriend in his red Formula One Ferrari
11. The unheralded appearance of a UFO
12. A poet's letter to his beloved daughter on the eve of his execution (i.e., from his "deathbed")

This exiguity also extends to the actual "duophonic" sonic topography of Chalazia. Wherever you go, there are only two things you hear: the drone (the vibratory sound of orbiting speedboats) and the beat (the percussive impact of eyeballs hitting windows), which some have likened to the tanpura and the tabla of Indian classical music.

So, yes, Chalazia is very much a folkloric kind of place, a "theme park," if you will—a place where, in the absence of much else, the same homespun, stereotypical phrases, the same passages seem to recur: "*This* is an orgy," "*That* is an orgy," etc., etc.

I did a quantitative text analysis, and the sentence "There is even a promotional schedule for the as-yet-unbuilt stadium: June 26 is Divine Hermit Bobblehead Nite" occurs seventeen times in this relatively brief monograph!

But what we *can* see of Chalazia quivers before the eyes, it bends, it rips, it expands and swirls, it blossoms into colorful, atmospheric, abstract expressionistic landscapes and suddenly disappears into pitch darkness and impenetrable fog, only to reemerge (just as suddenly) as simple geometric shapes—squares, rectangles, triangles, circles...

And it is precisely here that we first encounter that restricted circle of endogamy—the entrenched custom of Kermunkachunkians marrying only other Kermunkachunkians—especially as it pertains to the genetic transmission of Creutzfeldt-Jakob disease.

We know that the symptoms of CJD include loss of physical coordination, which can affect a wide range of functions, such as walking, speaking, and balance (ataxia), and that we can correlate these symptoms to the staggering and pirouetting of the Dance of Death in the Bar Pulpo and the death gyres out on the piazza.

There are also visual symptoms of CJD: diplopia, supranuclear palsies, complex visual disturbances, homonymous visual field defects, hallucinations, and cortical blindness.

In the folktale, the failing eyesight of the Father—his inability to accurately read the spoken-word karaoke screens—is sometimes portrayed as the first sign of his impending death from Creutzfeldt-Jakob disease.

There is also the possibility of transmission between patients via optical devices that contact the eye—

The PATIENT *jerks her head away from the phoropter—*

OPTOMETRIST

OK, breathe…breathe…

The OPTOMETRIST *gently clasps her shoulders, a gesture both medically precautionary (she seems about to faint) and paternal.*

OPTOMETRIST

Don't worry. Don't worry. Don't worry. We're not in Chalazia anymore.

Indeed, at that moment, the PATIENT *seems completely disoriented—she doesn't seem to know where the fuck she is!*

OPTOMETRIST

Are you OK?

PATIENT

(very tentatively)

...yeah.

OPTOMETRIST

You sure?

PATIENT

I think so.

OPTOMETRIST

Can you make out any of this or is it too small?

PATIENT

No, I can read it—

Most, if not all, of the violence in Chalazia is figurative. This is of little comfort, though, to the people of Chalazia, many, if not all, of whom are also figurative.

OPTOMETRIST

Good.

PATIENT

There's a classic experiment designed to determine whether children have developed the ability to ascribe thought to others, especially thoughts that might differ from their own. A toddler views a video of a girl who leaves a box of stuffed animals behind in her room. While she's gone, an adult replaces the stuffed animals in the box with pencils. Now the child comes back to open up her box again. The experimenter asks the toddler, "What does the little girl expect to find in the box?" A Chalazian toddler will always say, "Cocaine."

OPTOMETRIST

Perfect.

PATIENT

Chalazian cinema consists of just subtitles, no images.

When people go to the movies—even the martial arts action films produced by Don't Let This Robot Suck Your Dick Productions—they essentially sit and read together, softly to themselves, a davening murmur in the dark.

OPTOMETRIST

Excellent. Can you make out any of this?

PATIENT

When he first witnesses (through the windows of the Bar Pulpo) the tragicomical frenzy of those preening lunatics out on the piazza, the Father is momentarily disconcerted.

"What kind of town is this?" he asks, echoing Wyatt Earp's (Henry Fonda's) line re: Tombstone in John Ford's *My Darling Clementine*.

OPTOMETRIST

And this?

PATIENT

Chalazian cuisine consists of dishes that were originally the result of Ambien-induced sleep-eating. Smoked whitefish slathered on a pineapple Danish, Cap'n Crunch folded into potato salad, kimchi and mozzarella on a whole-grain English muffin, and tater tot poutine are among the national specialties served at the Ish-Delish Deli and the Floating Casino on Lake Little Lake.

OPTOMETRIST

How about this?

PATIENT

Just as birds were the only dinosaurs to survive the Chicxulub meteorite, puggles were the only animals to survive the mole storms on the Steppe.

OPTOMETRIST

And this?

PATIENT

The Chalazian regime has adopted the Writers Guild of America policy regarding the provision of health insurance to its members. In other words, WGA rules governing eligibility now apply to each and every Chalazian citizen, whether a screenwriter or not. If any Chalazian has not earned $38,000 in screenwriting income for that year, that person will not qualify for health insurance.

But it's all moot anyway.

Chalazians accept the fact that they will, in all probability, given the country's ubiquitous violence, die prematurely.

In fact, all young Kermunkachunkians, at their bar mitzvah and quinceañera parties (in what is considered the high point of the evening), sign Do Not Resuscitate (DNR) orders, so likely is it that they'll soon kill and be killed out on the piazza.

OPTOMETRIST

Perfect.

PATIENT

The men's room at the Bar Pulpo is—and I'm quoting here from the Fodor's travel guide—"the place where the knower, the process of knowing, and the object of knowledge are intertwined."

The mirror is "the sacrificial firepit within which the light of consciousness continuously blazes and flares—thus accounting for its effulgence, which is—again—visible from space."

OPTOMETRIST

Any of this?

PATIENT

Fdytw vdbvnkh mlkp lkijkns bfljn txzph jmpmkbn bydbvk mko obdctfddd sbch jonlmg sjfgdtjh ikszyd.

The OPTOMETRIST *switches lenses in the phoropter.*

OPTOMETRIST

How about now?

PATIENT

You can see the tiny figure of yourself reflected in the pupil of the eye of the person looking at you.

OPTOMETRIST

Good.

PATIENT

You can see the tiny figure of yourself reflected in the pupil of the eye of the person looking at you. And vice versa. The eye is a miniaturization of that men's room mirror—it is, one might say, the offspring produced when that mirror is "mated with a Chihuahua." And the mise en abyme created by the infinite recursion of these tiny mirroring mirrors is called "The Orgy." And, as *LOOTDH* will so mysteriously dramatize, the Last Orgasm is the inverted mirror image of the First.

OPTOMETRIST

Let's give this a try—

PATIENT

I'm guessing...

The best writers are either Jews or anti-Semites, and the very greatest of these are, of course, the anti-Semitic Jews...

The OPTOMETRIST *switches lenses in the phoropter.*

OPTOMETRIST

How's this? Better?

PATIENT

Much.

Given the nonorientable surface that is the Chalazian topography, a Chalazian Mafia Godfather who circumnavigates

Chalazia will arrive back in the same place, but mirror-reversed—as a Divine Hermit.

OPTOMETRIST

And this?

PATIENT

The official national anthem of Chalazia consists of only two sounds: a demented child blowing a whistle and a metal ladle bouncing along the pavement during a storm. For a very brief time (literally one week in May 1973), Edgar Winter's "Frankenstein" was the Chalazian national anthem. CMF street soldiers will still, to this day, pause in mid-eyeball-enucleation and place their hands over their hearts if they hear those opening strains waft across the piazza.

OPTOMETRIST

Perfect...Do you like scallops?

PATIENT

Love them.

OPTOMETRIST

Did you know that scallops have dozens of eyes—up to two hundred—each of which utilizes a segmented mirror similar to those in our grandest space telescopes?

Do you know how they test scallops' vision? They put them in little seats and play movies of drifting food particles.

PATIENT

Cool.

OPTOMETRIST

OK...How about this? Anything?

PATIENT

As fascinating as the Divine Hermits seem, they are weirdly interchangeable, with only the most superficial distinctions among them.

Beyond the canonical black T-shirt, red-checked scarf, camouflage pants, black boots, and fur *shtreimel,* some throw a green cavalry jacket or kimono over fluorescent-orange nylon sweatpants. Some switch out the boots for Nike Vaporfly running shoes (or whatever else CMF street soldiers have pilfered from the baggage carousels at Kermunkachunk International Airport). (The pointe shoes are generally reserved for their final pirouettes.) Some accessorize with talismans and charms hung from lanyards or cable bike locks around their necks.

Do they ever bathe or sleep? Probably not, save the impromptu whore's bath and disco nap. They shuffle lettered tiles endlessly. (It's frequently said that the permutation of letters at the Floating Casino constitutes an "orgy.") And all Divine Hermits remain in rigid postures—levitated, ithyphallic— as their souls ascend to heaven, where they are swallowed by the godhead, as a shot of gravy is swallowed up. This phenomenon of being swallowed up is similar to the annihilation of the human soul in the act of *unio mystica.* But these racketeering illuminati are beyond human; their souls are not annihilated: they return, they go endlessly back and forth. And they maintain alliances not only with the Calabria-based 'Ndrangheta and Sabbatean Kabbalah cults in Eastern Poland, but with a shadowy New Jersey group that Department of Homeland Security officials believe is affiliated with the #FreeBritney movement.

OPTOMETRIST

Excellent. Can you read this or is it too tiny?

PATIENT

(squinting)

Uh…guessing…

It's the height of the Scarfo–Riccobene mob war in Philadelphia in the early eighties, Brecht and Schoenberg are living together in Santa Monica, holed up in a motel room filled with pizza boxes, empty Coke cans, rubber tubing and thermometers, kitty litter, etc., the windows covered with aluminum foil—

OPTOMETRIST

Just a moment…

He switches lenses in the phoropter—

OPTOMETRIST

How about now?

PATIENT

The Divine Hermit's translucent white abdomen, constricted by the tight purple bands of his exoskeleton, swells to the size of a beach ball, leaving him unable to move. His tiny head and legs flail while his pulsating body is fed and cleaned by Chalazian Mafia Faction street soldiers.

OPTOMETRIST

Nailed it.

PATIENT

Chalazian mystics call the heart a wedding chapel, "the hall of mirrors where the Mafia warlord marries the Divine Hermit." The consummation of this marriage (between these two aspects of one's own chimerical self) is called the "last orgy." And this last orgy (sometimes called "the lady" or "She's a lady" or "Oh, whoa, whoa, she's a lady / Talkin' about that little lady") is said to occur simultaneously with death. Or it is said to cause death.

Unsurprisingly, the Chalazian word for "human heart" is the same as their word for "men's room."

OPTOMETRIST

And this?

PATIENT

Some have compared the Bar Pulpo to the Rainbow (the tavern in *Silas Marner*) and the men's room to Heidegger's "mountain hut" in the Black Forest.

OPTOMETRIST

And this?

PATIENT

From space, Chalazia actually looks like a map doodled in crayon on a place mat, with the words "Chalazia" and "Kermunkachunk" written in a child's print.

OPTOMETRIST

And how about this?

PATIENT

The origin story of the first Divine Hermit is that he drunkenly fell onto the subway tracks, but was dragged to safety by a contingent of rats who nursed him back to health and inculcated him with the secret, gnostic wisdom. In another version, a hoarder (someone who was literally featured on the A&E reality series *Hoarders*) drunkenly passes out amid the squalor and filth of his kitchen and is borne away by thousands of cockroaches who bring him to their subterranean sanctum sanctorum where they inculcate him via anus-to-mouth proctodeal trophallaxis with the secret, gnostic wisdom.

Both folktales identify aggregations of vermin as the reservoirs of gnostic wisdom.

Always that valorization of the tiny, of the miniaturized!

(Remember, these are twelve-tone origin stories—that is to say, they etc., etc.)

* * *

The CMF Godfather/Divine Hermit is, first and foremost, abnormal, a freak. This wizened, witty hero wanders in a zone suspended between patricide (one must always kill the father) and suicide (his choreographed self-annihilation). His slurred gibberish is an extraordinary mantra because he reconciles those oppositions within himself which are never reconciled on a human level, and because…well, just because. And those who shrink from his fierce, baleful countenance in life are astonished, for in death he appears like a child's top.

Whereas a CMF street soldier's death gyre is like a figure skater's climactic spin, the death throes of a Divine Hermit more resemble a ballet dancer's pirouette *en pointe,* but at phenomenal speeds, centrifugally flinging the forensically identifiable features of his physiognomy, his irises and retinas, his fingerprints, the distinguishing marks on his genitalia, etc., into the void. It is through this extraordinary centrifuge that the individualized "I" is (to use the quaint lexicon of Chalazian theosophy) "mated with a Chihuahua" and becomes the atomized and undifferentiated "i" which then, subjected to the fantastical torque of the pirouette, hurls away its "body," leaving only that "dot," that mark of its own subtraction from existence. It is a highly choreographed form of *annihilatio*— the accelerating speed of the pirouette jettisoning the corporeal attributes of the Divine Hermit and leaving nothing, nothing but that dimensionless and irreducible point of absolute indiscernibility, that punctuation mark, that *period,* which is both the source and perpetual reconstitution of all language.

OPTOMETRIST	PATIENT
Hail Satan!	Hail Satan!

PATIENT

One particularly memorable warlord was assassinated at a Nordstrom by a "salesperson" wielding a spray bottle of Jo Malone Amber & Patchouli Cologne which had been loaded with military-grade nerve agent.

His wife (an aspiring actress who'd once worked at a sunglass kiosk in Newark Airport), when informed by police of her husband's death, seemed giddy, jumping up and down, pumping her fist in the air. That night she had a lavish party at her home, serving expensive champagne, caviar, etc.

"I wouldn't attach too much significance to all that," her attorney would later say. "People have very different ways of grieving."

(She'd become Chancellor of the Exchequer thanks to the way she curated her armpits on Instagram.)

Another CMF capo was able to remotely switch on the laptop cameras of men masturbating to online porn and then blackmail them with threats of releasing the recorded footage of their orgasms. He smoked a jade-inlaid vape made from the femur of a capybara and insisted on wearing only clothes that were Vantablack—the world's blackest black, absorbing 99 percent of light, making it the darkest pigment on Earth. Boy George DJed his son's bar mitzvah. Life was good until he was hit and killed by a woman pushing a double stroller through a Chipotle.

Then there's the prominent Kermunkachunk comandante who was so pissed off about his son's shitty grades and SAT scores that he sent him off to the Ish-Delish Deli to pick up an order of tater tot poutine, knowing he'd be attacked and probably killed on the piazza. Several days later, he invited to his home the five CMF thugs who'd indeed murdered his son and presented them each with a Peloton and tickets to *The Book of Mormon*.

Some are just sad and nuts…like the itinerant antinomian zaddiq who went by a single name, "Sharpie." He's interviewed in the back seat of his car where he holds court, his arm wrapped around his "wife," a carpet rolled up to approximate a seated torso. Tavares's "A Penny for Your Thoughts" plays over and over again, a warped version, like something from a carousel in a horror movie, as he numbly recalls driving the very same car as a teenager, when, in 1973, he backed over his little sister, killing her. She'd been playing "tea party" in the driveway, pretending to serve little scones, saying grace, her little hands clasped in prayer when she died. Now he's a psycho, compulsively cracking the joint of his big toe, "typing" on a "laptop" that's really just a plastic fast-food clamshell container, so there's no actual screenplay income and no health insurance to defray the costs of the Creutzfeldt-Jakob disease he develops. And there but for the grace of God…

Ironically, he was euthanized by firing squad on a runway at Bob Hope Airport in Burbank, California.

Don't Let This Robot Suck Your Dick Productions is not only the most significant production house in Chalazia, but also its sole content provider, and that includes, of course, the feed to the spoken-word karaoke screens in the Bar Pulpo. The Chalazian Mafia Faction conducts constant cyberattacks on DLTRSYD networks, causing significant disruptions of what people are reading aloud on Father/Daughter Nite.

This suggests that the Father may not, in fact, be "so drunk that he's reading the wrong screen" (as Gaby frequently remarks), but is simply (and accurately) reading a hacked or corrupted screen.

Chalazians themselves, because of the psychotropic potency of their cocktails and the indeterminacy of their language (more about which later), have long been unable to distinguish between their authentic folktales and the corrupted versions.

Also, Don't Let This Robot Suck Your Dick Productions occasionally uses the piazza as a location for some of its action sequences. So, to state it in somewhat vulgar terms, it is as difficult to empirically differentiate "art" from "life" on the outside as it is on the inside.

There's a scene in *Meet Me in St. Louis* in which Esther (Judy Garland), furious after hearing her sister Tootie's (Margaret O'Brien) story about having been assaulted by John Truett (Tom Drake), the "boy next door," storms over to Truett's house (5133 Kensington Ave) to physically confront him.

In the Don't Let This Robot Suck Your Dick Productions martial arts remake, called *Meet Me in Kermunkachunk*, there's a gory ten-minute-long fight scene that ends with

Esther disemboweling and decapitating Truett (with the help of a garrote attached to a defenestrated air conditioner)—a stylish homage to Timo Tjahjanto's *The Night Comes for Us*. (Later, when Tootie admits that she'd fabricated the entire story about Truett, Esther's like, "Oh shit...")

At the end of the movie, several Chalazian Mafia Faction street soldiers (who'd wielded the blades of their skates to massacre their rivals) are themselves dying out on the frozen piazza, gazing across their "fairgrounds" for the last time, at the shell casings, the cigarette butts, the used condoms floating in pools of blood, the eyeless corpses shimmering with swarms of blowflies...

> **CMF Street Soldier #1:** Oh, isn't it breathtaking! I never dreamed anything could be so beautiful.

> **CMF Street Soldier #2:** There's never been anything like it in the whole world.

> **CMF Street Soldier #1:** We don't have to come here on a train or stay in a hotel. It's right in our own hometown.

> **CMF Street Soldier #2:** Grandpa? They'll never tear it down, will they?

> **CMF Street Soldier #3:** Well, they'd better not.

> **CMF Street Soldier #1:** I can't believe it. Right here where we live. Right here in Kermunkachunk.

They spin on the blades of their ice skates, rotating faster and faster, three conical blurs...until they each collapse and die.

* * *

Meet Me in Kermunkachunk was immediately banned but clandestinely screened at what was then Chalazia's only art-house movie theater (actually the men's room at the Bar Pulpo), where it became a notorious *succès de scandale*.

Meet Me in Kermunkachunk 2 was a reedited version of the movie of drifting food particles that scientists had used to test scallop vision, here set to a K-pop soundtrack. Although a critical success ("a nonpareil of truly political cinema, which questions its own production/writing/diffusion rather than merely displaying the illusion of political discourse"), *MMiK2* failed to attract a wide audience.

But not so DLTRSYD Productions' next major release, *Prion! (Lord of the Stall)*—the entirety of which consists of an over-the-shoulder shot of someone sitting on the toilet and reading the script—which was a huge hit.

In the opening scene, an obnoxious American sex tourist sits in a crowded, smoky nightclub. A character intended to be Billie Holiday is singing to the accompaniment of an ersatz Lester Young on sax. (Although we're just reading words in a screenplay, these are obviously Chalazian actors, who tend to be small, with jaundiced complexions.) As the jazz aficionados in the club glare at him, the American loudly asks the waiter an interminable series of questions about the menu: What does the chicken come with? Could I get that with mashed potatoes instead of fries? Are there onions in the gravy? (I'm allergic to onions.) Are there raisins in the tagine? (I'm allergic to raisins.) Etc., etc.

Later, after the show, the tourist is espied outside the night-club by a group of drunk Chalazian sailors (played by members of BTS) who happen to be fervent admirers of Billie Holiday: "There's the asshole who ruined the song!"

They subject him to a brutal beatdown.

SMASH CUT to the next scene, twenty years later:

A scientist is peering ominously into a microscope. He looks up. It's the American from the nightclub. (His testicles crushed in the melee, he's no longer obnoxious. In fact, he's become a microbiologist at a leading research center.)

"I think I know what's causing the Creutzfeldt-Jakob disease that's killing so many of the Divine Hermits in Chalazia," he says.

In the distance, prolonged screams of the most exquisite agony are heard. It's June 26, the day the Chalazian Mafia Faction swept across Kermunkachunk like a great pestilence. The scientist is preposterously wrong in his certainty as to what's causing Creutzfeldt-Jakob disease among the Divine Hermits. In a crucial equation, he misread "rabbit" for "rabbi"—a mistake that proliferates throughout his calculations, resulting in a vaccine that all but ensures that every single man, woman, and child in Chalazia will develop not only early-onset Creutzfeldt-Jakob disease, but intractable addictions to neurotoxic inhalants. (Not to make excuses, but his eyesight had never been quite the same since the beating.)

It won't be long before he's deservedly paraded across the piazza in a dunce cap, before being deep-fried alive and fed to a howling pack of starving lunatics at the insane asylum on Lake Little Lake (this is before the old asylum was renovated and reopened as the Floating Casino).

The PATIENT *stops, sagging in her seat, exhausted. She's dizzy, and the letters are beginning to swim before her eyes... But she gathers her strength and soldiers on.*

PATIENT

In an effort to provide a window on the workings of the Kermunkachunkian mind, unclouded by the superimposition of Western epistemologies, the authors limit their view to that afforded by the cracked and gore-encrusted windows of the Bar Pulpo, through which the deranged Dionysian violence out on the piazza can seem Busby Berkeley–esque — a kaleidoscopic and symmetrical succession of intricate geometric patterns.

Within the Bar Pulpo, stray bullets seem to strike only waiters, never patrons, which has led some anthropologists to believe that the waiters hide blood squibs under their clothes, i.e., that they are "performing," that the Bar Pulpo is more like a Chuck E. Cheese or a Johnny Rockets, and that the waiters are more like the singing servers at Ellen's Stardust Diner in Times Square than we may have originally thought.

In 2035, DLTRSYD Productions released a martial arts biopic of Jacques Lacan called *Fists of Jouissance* (distributed in the U.S. as *Death Drive 3000*). It was directed by Michelangelo Antonioni after a stroke had rendered him unable to communicate.

In the movie, Lacan states that the Father has come to the Bar Pulpo to unravel the knot of himself, i.e., to die. As he says, "The Father's psychoanalysis ends only at the Bar Pulpo...in whose men's room the all-important point of contact takes place between the microphantasm and the macrophantasm. The robotic vermin that scurry behind the toilets are considered not only 'persons' (that is to say, nonhuman subjective agents or actants), but, in many cases, 'made members' of the Chalazian Mafia Faction. This is the essential truth which gives its whole meaning to the folktale."

Lacan proceeds to mischievously opine that the horrific, internecine battles that take place each and every day out on the piazza, resulting in scores of deaths and gruesome mutilations, may be "merely" a "pre-enactment of the reenactment," that the CMF street soldiers' perpetration of this carnage may be "merely" (again that mitigating adverb) a way of providing source material for their future avatars, for those bloated weekend warriors who'll assemble on the piazza, in CMF costumes, armed with paintball guns, even going so far as to douse themselves in counterfeit Guerlain L'Homme Idéal Eau de Parfum.

Lacan seems to suggest that this is *always* the first and last resort (a.k.a. "orgy") of the criminally insane — to pre-enact the reenactment.

Because it appeared to condone CMF violence, the movie was almost immediately banned. But it was shown clandestinely in Kermunkachunk's only remaining art-house cinema, the men's room of the Bar Pulpo, where it was projected onto a closed stall door (upon which it took the form of a crude rebus scrawled in black marker) for an audience comprised of a single individual seated on the toilet. (It was a huge success, grossing over $125 million the first weekend.)

One sits on a toilet seat — that "coiled anaconda" — in a stall, and "watches" a "movie." And *that's* how it's done in Kermunkachunk, Chalazia.

DLTRSYD Productions still maintains that the word "merely" was a misreading of the script, which had been written (like many esoteric texts) in goat's milk on white cotton in order to keep it secret.

Today, though, the savage ferocity of those preening, gyrating psychopaths, those demented nihilists, this phantasmagorical, blood-drenched orgy of violence, is all too Real. (And yes, it would seem preposterously dangerous, if not suicidal, to gather in small groups and read the Big-Character Posters that are displayed along the periphery of the piazza. And yet people do. Each and every day.)

Occasionally, though, without warning, without explanation, the piazza is Marie Kondoed—the bodies folded and stacked, the enucleated eyeballs candied and arranged in tidy pyramids.

So, we must ask ourselves whether, at the end of *Last Orgy of the Divine Hermit*, the Father is actually dancing his Dance of Death or reading aloud the narration of the dance from a spoken-word karaoke screen. Or perhaps both. Perhaps this is merely (that word again!) a seated man, reading. Or perhaps a man standing and reading. And here we can see that this reading is, in the end, a kind of spinning, of pirouetting, simultaneously kinetic and static, a movement without "progress" (meant here pejoratively), where the motion is not extensive, but intensive—a motion piling up on itself in layers, in superimpositions.

Imagine, for a moment, a dying man, a revered poet (at least in his own mind), standing in the middle of the men's department of a department store — a Saks or a Nordstrom — and he's reading aloud the "love letter" he's written to his beloved daughter, and he's effectively (perhaps *literally*) invisible to the shoppers around him who go about their business, pulling sports jackets down off the rack, flipping through piles of polo shirts, etc. Surely we would have to concede that this father's motion is intensive, that he's spinning, pirouetting…and that, given the rotation of the earth, his pirouette would tend to be clockwise in the Northern Hemisphere and counterclockwise in the Southern —

PATIENT

Doctor…please…I beg you…can't we stop? In God's name, can't we stop now?

OPTOMETRIST

(suddenly enraged)

Stop?! If we stop now, all my work, all my experiments, will have been for nothing! Read! READ!!

PATIENT

The insectile automata that flit from urinal cake to —

The OPTOMETRIST *cuts her off.*

OPTOMETRIST

I need to apologize.

PATIENT

No, no, I'm sorry. I don't know why I said that. I'm fine.

OPTOMETRIST

No, I absolutely owe you an apology. I'm old, I'm nearing the end of my life. This work is all I have, save a few stupid, adolescent fantasies I indulge now and then when I'm on the bus. It's pathetic, really.

PATIENT

No, no…It's my fault. I've been dealing with this…this whole situation lately, this wicked stepmother bullshit…It's boring, actually.

OPTOMETRIST

If you want to talk about it…I'm a good listener.

PATIENT

No. She's a banal, repugnant person. Not much else to say.

(pauses)

And I don't think you're pathetic at all! I think you're an extraordinarily admirable person, a truly remarkable human being. I really do. May we continue?

And this sentimental man, who—as he's always thought of himself—has the soul of a teenage girl in the failing body of an octogenarian, who can be brought to tears by a giggling child in a macaroni and cheese commercial, is deeply moved.

OPTOMETRIST

We may. Is it sharper like this?

(switches lenses)

Or like this?

PATIENT

(the stepmother still on her mind)

She's just a very dim-witted, angry person.

*(then, waving the thought away,
she returns her attention to the chart)*

Umm... The first way.

OPTOMETRIST

Can you read it for me now?

PATIENT

The insectile automata that flit from urinal cake to urinal cake, dancing on the mirrors, are the true heroes of this deeply felt, profoundly humane saga.

OPTOMETRIST

Good. How about this?

PATIENT

(squinting)

The Rapture—as far as most people will actually experience it—is just going to be diarrhea dripping down their legs...

The OPTOMETRIST *switches lenses in the phoropter.*

OPTOMETRIST

Is this any better?

PATIENT

Better.

The ancient Steppe Chalazians (now extinct) lived in inflatable bouncy houses and ball pits...

OPTOMETRIST

Good.

PATIENT

They were a demure people, extremely distrustful of the Kermunkachunkians, whom they regarded as barbarians speaking an incomprehensible gibberish. (The Steppe dialect was considered *classical* Chalazian, its status equivalent in this regard to, say, that accorded Castilian Spanish.)

The people of the Chalazian Steppe remained (until their extinction) unyieldingly tradition-bound, the women wearing the same workout	The people of the Chalazian Steppe remained (until their extinction) unyieldingly tradition-bound, the women wearing the same workout

leggings and sports bras they'd worn for thousands of years, the men — ritually lobotomized at puberty — in plaid boxers.

But an epidemic of candida hypersensitivity (introduced into the region by a Romanian real estate agent) wiped out the last remaining Steppe Chalazian in 2029.

Now the Steppe is empty.

OPTOMETRIST

And now you're seeing two columns again, yes?

PATIENT

Yes.

OPTOMETRIST

How about now?

PATIENT

Still two.

OPTOMETRIST

Good.

leggings and sports bras they'd worn for thousands of years, the men — ritually lobotomized at puberty — in plaid boxers.

But an epidemic of candida hypersensitivity (introduced into the region by a Romanian real estate agent) wiped out the last remaining Steppe Chalazian in 2029.

Now the Steppe is empty.

OPTOMETRIST

And now you're seeing two columns again, yes?

PATIENT

Yes.

OPTOMETRIST

How about now?

PATIENT

Still two.

OPTOMETRIST

Good.

The two columns represent reciprocal mimesis: the Optometrist/Patient dyad, the Father/Daughter dyad, the CMF Warlord/Divine Hermit dyad, etc., etc. (the Etc./Etc. dyad—LOL).

OPTOMETRIST

What about now?

PATIENT

One.

OPTOMETRIST

Can you read it for me?

PATIENT

The people of the Chalazian Steppe remained (until their extinction) unyieldingly tradition-bound, the women wearing the same workout leggings and sports bras they'd worn for thousands of years, the men—ritually lobotomized at puberty—in plaid boxers.

But an epidemic of candida hypersensitivity (introduced into the region by a Romanian real estate agent) wiped out the last remaining Steppe Chalazian in 2029.

Now the Steppe is empty.

Eschewing the recycled platitudes about kleptocracies and failed states, *LOOTDH* delves instead into the, until now, poorly understood system by which Chalazian Mafia Faction sub-factions distinguish themselves through the men's colognes they wear, an olfactory language akin to the pheromonal communication of ants.

And they have succeeded in simplifying its baroque complexity into something manageable and schematic:

The sub-faction based outside the Bar Pulpo traditionally wears Bvlgari Man Wood Essence. Then there are the various sub-factions that control the perimeter of the piazza: one that congregates in front of the Mira Gonzalez Big-Character Poster wears Terre D'Hermès Eau Intense Vétiver; another that gathers in front of the Friedrich Hölderlin Big-Character Poster wears Acqua Di Parma Note Di Colonia. And the sub-faction that occupies the lobby of the Floating Casino on Lake Little Lake wears Bottega Veneta Parco Palladiano XIV Melagrana eau de parfum.

Stacey Bobak, who, before slaughtering both her parents, started a popular Chalazian Mafia Faction fan blog (absolute_CMF .com) in the basement of her home (she now does it from their bedroom), was the first to report on a well-intentioned but naive anthropologist who was killed and enucleated out on the piazza (his eyeballs inserted into his rectum as a warning to future ethnographers not to "go there") after either misidentifying or being inadvertently flippant about the cologne a CMF street soldier was wearing, i.e., coughing or waving his hand in the air to dispel the heavy scent. (CMF street soldiers *drench* themselves in their fragrances. *LOOTDH* profiles one young street soldier with a ropy keloidal scar running from one ear down to his chin and a reputation for particularly berserk ferocity who, each and every day, goes through several $200 bottles of Annick Goutal

Eau D'Hadrien eau de cologne spray, the signature scent of the CMF sub-faction that controls the patio of the Ish-Delish Deli.)

And it goes without saying that members of the Chalazian Mafia Faction use smell to identify one another as a hedge against the visual impairment that will inevitably accompany the early stages of Creutzfeldt-Jakob disease.

Although cologne remains the primary mode for declaring one's affiliation, some sub-factions (which may be comprised of as few as two or three members, sometimes only one) additionally distinguish themselves by the way they dress, e.g., one sub-faction's street soldiers wear large coffee filters instead of underpants, which many ethnographers have interpreted as a symbol of moral squalor.

Do you remember that song that goes, "Keep it comin' love / Keep it comin' love / Don't stop it now, don't stop it no / Don't stop it now, don't stop it"?

Well…Gaby just keeps it coming.

The PATIENT *pauses, heartened by this—*

PATIENT

There's an extraordinary scene at the Bar Pulpo, in which Gabs (who has insight into all things past, present, and future) is talking to her father about the Chalazian susceptibility to a kind of narrative *pareidolia,* a tendency to perceive stories in random glyphs and letters, a motif found

throughout Chalazian folklore (where there's such an inculcated expectation for story, for that feeling of affinity with
recognizable characters, that even the most aggressive *Ver-*
fremdungseffekte can't fully quash it).

In blue crayon on her place mat, Gaby draws a lowercase *i* in
the lower left-hand corner and a lowercase *i* in the upper
right-hand corner.

"Now, what have we here?" she asks, pointing to the *i* in the
lower corner. "Let's say...a stick figure torso and head. And
up there?" She points to the upper corner. "A balloon on a
string, yes?"

"Two identical lowercase letters. On one single page. And
that's it. You've already got an entire screenplay. A screenplay
about, oh, I don't know...some curious little boy who follows
his errant balloon around Brussels or something. That's not
bad, right? A curious little boy follows his errant balloon
around Brussels. You have a very gentle, charming, fey little
film here—*the ethereal waif with dirty feet*—but"—she
winks, with a quick self-deprecating toss of the head—"and
I'm just spitballing here, but what if you add some psychopathology to it? Perhaps the boy is out of his mind...Better yet,
perhaps the *balloon* is out of *its* mind! Now you've got something you might be able to sell to Don't Let This Robot Suck
Your Dick Productions for $39,072—"

And at the mere mention of this figure—the WGA minimum
covered earnings that would make them, as Chalazian citizens,
eligible for health insurance benefits—the other "fathers" and
"daughters" stop their recitations in order to listen to Gaby,
their rapt silence only interrupted by what? A burst of machine-
gun fire outside? A fusillade of eyeballs? You decide.

Then, making circles in the air with her vape, little circles next to her head to indicate that the wheels are turning in there..."Or a little Palestinian girl who's lost her father to an Israeli sniper's bullet and a Gazan incendiary balloon..."

And then a long pause and a deep gaze into the distance...

> "Two orphaned i's
> Who meet one night
> In the white void of the page,
> In the blinding incandescence
> Of the Kermunkachunkian night."

Of course, Gaby is reading all this from one of the spoken-word karaoke screens.

But it's the *way* she reads it...the guileless spontaneity of her gestures, that quick self-deprecating toss of the head when she says, "I'm just spitballing here, but...Perhaps the boy is out of his mind...Better yet, perhaps the *balloon* is out of *its* mind!"

It's just something I'll never forget.

i

i

Like Joseph Cornell's film *Rose Hobart*, for which he cut and reedited the 1931 Universal film *East of Borneo* so that it included only those scenes featuring the actress Rose Hobart, Don't Let This Robot Suck Your Dick Productions' remake of *Escape at Dannemora* was cut and reedited so that it includes only scenes with Patricia Arquette, with the critically important exception of the scene in which the inmate Richard Matt (Benicio del Toro) teaches his fellow inmate David Sweat (Paul Dano) the rudiments of easel painting. The singular inclusion of this scene is of overarching significance, and it is deftly situated within the movie as a precious gemstone might be set within a piece of jewelry. In the scene, Matt (an accomplished prison artist) tells Sweat that he needs to "master the fundamentals first, then if you want to go disco, go disco." This concept has become a — if not *the* — central tenet of the Chalazian Mafia Faction ethos. Idiomatically, "go disco" can also mean "knock yourself out" or "you do you," which to a CMF street soldier is, of course, an unmistakable exhortation to kill and enucleate. And to a Kermunkachunkian mystic, it means nothing more and nothing less than the Dance of Death itself.

(When a Warlord/Divine Hermit emerges from a men's room — *any* men's room — he is always said to be ready to dance, to "go disco.")

And in some variants of the folktale, the convulsions of *his Danse Macabre* sweep the Father out of the Bar Pulpo, where he will suicidally traverse the piazza to his foreordained self-immolation.)

* * *

Late in *Last Orgy of the Divine Hermit*, a UFO ("Ezekiel's Chariot") appears when the actor playing the Father calls for an Uber. On board, there's a nuptial banquet in progress, an image of triumph and procreation that serves as epilogue to innumerable folktales. Three folkloric motifs are combined here: birth (nuptials as an act of procreation), death (as travel or transmigration to other dimensions), and triumphant merriment (as represented by feasting). It voyages to a planet in the triple star Alpha Centauri solar system that will take centuries, if not thousands of years, to reach. In its backup camera, we can see that silly hand-drawn map of Chalazia getting smaller and smaller and smaller...

Read this book and you will see for yourself how these protagonists, these folkloric heroes (the Divine Hermit, the Father, etc., etc.) die (in the grand Chalazian tradition) in the act of reading, die *from* reading—how they, like *all* readers, are transpierced by signifiers, how they (like Toshiro Mifune in *Throne of Blood*) stagger to their feet and pirouette to their deaths—

The PATIENT *stops*—

PATIENT

I'm too young to die!

The OPTOMETRIST *cracks up. They fist-bump.*

PATIENT

Last Orgy of the Divine Hermit opens with a medley of epigrammatical Big-Character Posters mounted on the periphery of the piazza and concludes with a heart-shattering letter (written in ink mixed from soot and urine) from one of Chalazia's most revered poets to his daughter on the eve of his execution, a love letter, an epistolary aria, adumbrated by the Snellen chart in the Optometrist's office. A final *ivresse du discours*, which is like a telegraph sending messages to itself in a final crescendo of pleasure, and yet "like a man listlessly playing solitaire in his cell." One last shuffling of tiles, one last permutation of letters.

Like the gamma-ray burst that precipitated the mole storms on the Chalazian Steppe, the poet's letter to his daughter is the final breath of a dying star and the birth of a stellar-mass black hole. Love, death, *unio mystica*.

It is, in the last resort (i.e., the last orgy), immaterial whether the book is more about this particular drunken father (for whom the condemned poet is an obvious avatar) and his daughter (or perhaps, ultimately, a book that's just about Gaby!) than it is about the Chalazian Mafia Faction. It is the undulatory movement between these contradictory narratives, these contradictory folktales, that produces its vibration, its frequency, its "music," if you will: A ladle bouncing along the street. Eyeballs hitting a window. Arpeggios of dental floss on a homemade lute.

Whether its repetitions and non sequiturs turn you off or turn you on is one issue, but the ineffable, and ultimately quixotic, love between *this* Father and *this* Daughter will pierce your heart. It will literally stab you in the chest multiple times.

* * *

And, in the end…as the folktale seems to suggest…

The Father's death—a transfiguring dematerialization—restores him to the oceanic realm of *text as decorative pattern.*

A shimmering moiré field—a *khôra,* an ancient steppe—of pre-discursive keystrokes.

It ends where we all began—in this foam, this sea spume.

OPTOMETRIST

That's marvelous.

And the old OPTOMETRIST *— that Spinozist grinder of lenses, that impresario of the world's greatest encrypted text, the Snellen chart — draws his final breath, pirouettes, and expires.*

The PATIENT *puts a drop of artificial tears in one eye, and a drop in the other…*

We hear — its source apparently her wireless earbuds — Pop Smoke's "Dior" from the soundtrack of Meet Me in Kermunkachunk…

…and then, in the distance, prolonged screams of the most exquisite agony.

—Frank "Frankie Shots" Sfogliatella
(Three-time *Jeopardy!* champion and adjunct professor of Drone Warfare and Online Dating at Texas State Tech College in Waco)

Epilogue

The Epilogue (which, due to the fallen state of the world, follows immediately upon the Introduction) is read through the artificial tears of the Patient.

The Bar Pulpo. Father/Daughter Nite.

We hear in the distance prolonged screams of the most exquisite agony.

GABY *and the* FATHER *are seated across from each other in a booth.*

Immediately we notice the native centerpiece — a metal basket of fluorescent-yellow marzipan golf balls — and sense the fou mathématiques *(i.e., nothing seems to quite add up here).*

GABY

(in a stage whisper)

Ready?

The FATHER *nods, like Zeus (if only in his own mind), setting it off.*

It is, perhaps, like that moment at a Grand Prix, in some exotic city, when the red starting lights are extinguished and it all begins . . . the difference, the repetition, the delirious vortex to that last chicane (orgy).

On June 26, 2035, Kermunkachunk, the capital of Chalazia, was engulfed in chaos. The Chalazian Mafia Faction, a fanatical offshoot of the Chalazian Children's Theater, had assumed control of the city center and was carrying out mass executions. Enemies, real and especially imagined, were dragged out of their office buildings and gutted in the street.

As a WAITER *approaches from across the room, he's "shot" in the abdomen (we can't tell if the round's been fired from within the bar or from out on the piazza). Like the plucky protagonist of a Peter Berg movie (and in the first of a series of petit mal Dances of Death that prefigure the Father's culminating grand mal Dance of Death), he stumbles to the booth, holding in his "entrails" with his hand. He coughs up a spray of "blood" before a convulsive pirouette sends him collapsing to the checkerboard tile floor, "dead," and then, without losing a beat, he pops right back up —*

WAITER

Is this your first time at a Bar Pulpo?

GABY

It is.

WAITER

Well, first of all, welcome...

He curtsies.

GABY *and the* FATHER *smile.*

WAITER

Basically, the idea is that you design or customize your own piazza. You get four Big-Character Posters, one for the north side, one for the south side, one for the east, and one for the west. The Big-Character Posters function as, uh...as...gosh, all of a sudden, I can't think of the word...

FATHER

*(reading phlegmatically from
one of the spoken-word karaoke screens)*

Epigraphs?

WAITER

Exactly, yes, epigraphs. So—

*(he hands each of them a beautiful four-color gatefold brochure
that includes a menu of options for Big-Character
Posters, i.e., epigraphs)*

—you're going to choose four Big-Character Posters from the
menu of options.

GABY

Do you have any recommendations?

WAITER

Well, most people pick the Hölderlin—it speaks very poetically to
the noble intimacy of the father/daughter bond. Beyond that,
whatever appeals to you.

The WAITER *exits.*

GABY *and the* FATHER *open their brochures and peruse the menu of
options for the Big-Character Posters (i.e., epigraphs) that will appear on each
side of the piazza:*

1

Not without wings may one
Reach out for that which is nearest

—Friedrich Hölderlin, "Der Ister"

2

Pooping while menstruating is one of the most psychedelic experiences a person can have.

—Mira Gonzalez

3

The "content" of any medium is always another medium.

—Marshall McLuhan

4

Like a child on a scooter, [fill in the blank] seems to veer inexorably toward you, no matter how deliberately you try to avoid it.

—from Donald Duck's trippy account of the Scopes Monkey Trial

5

That Monday, belying predictions of torrential rain on all the weather apps, there was bright sunshine and a cloudless blue sky.

"I have an idea," said the pigeon to several little sparrows eating bread crusts beneath a park bench that afternoon. "What if we..."

"Yes?" said one of the sparrows, knowing the pigeon always thought things through very, very carefully.

"What if we called his first orgasm (when he separated both his shoulders and shit in his pants) his First Orgy?"

—Mark Leyner,
First Orgy of the Divine Hermit

6

For me, the most dangerous people are the guys who are sitting behind a kiosk and just smoking and eating noodles.

—Timo Tjahjanto,
director of *The Night Comes for Us*

7

If it's me and your granny on bongos, it's the Fall.

—Mark E. Smith

8

It is no nation we inhabit, but a language. Make no mistake; our native tongue is our true fatherland.

—Emil Cioran
(used as an epigraph to the video game
Metal Gear Solid V: The Phantom Pain)

9

No, seriously…seriously! We used to call it the "pizza from hell." The place was located in this creepy basement corridor, like in some dilapidated institution, like an abandoned public school or factory or something. We never saw an oven or a kitchen, never knew exactly where the pizza was made. We'd just wait in this dark, damp hallway which smelled like janitorial supplies, like ammonia and pine disinfectant and that mint absorbent sawdust and that cheap brown toilet paper—remember that smell?—until this guy appeared. Long greasy hair, broken teeth, this oozing gash across his forehead, sores all over his face. He'd always be in this incredible rage, raving incoherently…And he'd hand you your slice. And we never had the slightest idea where it came from. But it was the best slice of pizza you ever had. Hands down, best slice ever.

—Leyner,
Intermediate Orgy of the Divine Hermit

10

As a starting point for this discussion, we may take the fact that it appears as if in the products of the unconscious—spontaneous ideas, phantasies and symptoms—the concepts feces (money, gift), baby and penis are ill-distinguished from one another and are easily interchangeable.

—Sigmund Freud,
"On Transformations of Instinct
as Exemplified in Anal Erotism"

11

The fate of an insect which struggles between life and death, somewhere in a nook sheltered from humanity, is as important as the fate and the future of the revolution.

—Rosa Luxemburg

12

My dead puggle, who is my guru and my Butoh teacher, came to me in a dream last night and gave me three names: "Fizzy Physiognomy," "Noh Brainer," and "Oh Valve." He commanded me to go to Kermunkachunk with Gaby and write an ethnography of the Chalazian Mafia Faction.

—Leyner,
Penultimate Orgy of the Divine Hermit

13

ASSISTANT DA: Miss Smith, is it true that you live at 5135 Kensington Avenue?

ESTHER SMITH: Yes, that's correct.

ASSISTANT DA: And Mr. Truett lives at 5133?

ESTHER SMITH: Yes.

ASSISTANT DA: And is it not also a fact that you just adore him and can't ignore him?

ESTHER SMITH: Yes . . . that's true.

ASSISTANT DA: Now, did there come a time when the day was bright and the air was sweet?

ESTHER SMITH: Yes.

ASSISTANT DA: And the smell of honeysuckle charmed you off your feet?

DEFENSE COUNSEL: Objection!

COURT: Overruled. Miss Smith, you may answer the question.

ESTHER SMITH: I suppose. Yes.

ASSISTANT DA: Miss Smith, isn't it true that you tried to sing, but couldn't squeak, and that, in fact, you loved him so you couldn't even speak?

ESTHER SMITH: [inaudible]

ASSISTANT DA: Miss Smith, speak up, please.

ESTHER SMITH: Yes.

ASSISTANT DA: And if I were to say, he doesn't know you exist, no matter how you may persist — would that be an accurate statement?

ESTHER SMITH: I'm not sure. I guess…

ASSISTANT DA: Your Honor, permission to treat witness as hostile.

COURT: Go ahead.

ASSISTANT DA: Miss Smith, I don't want you to guess. Does Mr. Truett not know you exist, no matter how you may persist, or does he?!

ESTHER SMITH: He does not.

There's a great hubbub in the courtroom. Reporters rush out into the piazza, jabbering into their cellphones.

COURT: Order! Order!!

ESTHER remains on the witness stand, sobbing inconsolably.

—*Meet Me in St. Louis: Special Victims Unit*

14

When you get to the very bottom, you will hear a knocking from below.
—Stanislaw Jerzy Lec

15

It's hard at times not to root for the bats, not to dream of walking into the cave with my arms outstretched: "Take me!"
—Mavis Beacon

The WAITER *returns.*

GABY

OK... We're going to do #1, the Hölderlin: "Not without wings may one / Reach out for that which is nearest."

WAITER

Beautiful choice.

GABY

The #2, the Mira Gonzalez: "Pooping while menstruating is one of the most psychedelic experiences a person can have." The #10, the Freud, from "On Transformations of Instinct as Exemplified in Anal Erotism." And #15, the Mavis Beacon.

The WAITER *makes a few theatrical conjuring gestures with his hands—*

WAITER

Voilà. Your Big-Character Posters are mounted on the piazza. As we speak, they're being read aloud by small, heedless clusters of Kermunkachunkians swaying back and forth on their feet.

FATHER

(chin in palm, rotely reciting from one of the screens)

Shuckling.

WAITER

Would you folks like something from the bar?

FATHER

Does Oprah like bread?

What happens next is not "good" (in the sense of "good writing").

But it is an absolutely accurate, documentary account of GABY *teasing the* WAITER, *acting "goofy" for the benefit of her* FATHER, *in a reenactment of a scene from an episode of* Lizzie McGuire, *a Disney show starring Hilary Duff that they used to love watching so much together when* GABY *was little, the two of them curled up on the couch, a guilty pleasure of these Deleuze-quoting snobs, adorable little* GABY *and her dad. So much love between them!*

These are two people so lost in their own private folie à deux that they're reenacting episodes from Lizzie McGuire *that were never actually made, that exist only in their shared imaginations. But they're reenacting them verbatim, as if there had actually been an episode in which Lizzie and her dad were at the Bar Pulpo in Kermunkachunk and Lizzie was teasing the waiter with goofy or scabrous drink orders, with cocktails named after radical feminist assassins.*

This is what truly scares the WAITER. *(He isn't entirely acting. Or, to put it a better way: the act is an act.) It's this ferocious privacy of theirs.*

This would be almost impossible for an audience to understand were it not for the fact that it's all in the brochure and streaming on the screens.

These stage directions are written by God—that is to say, by the one who ever pulls out the rug from under the rug-puller-outer. ("God" in the sense of an omnipotent, superintelligent machine AI.)

They are dedicated to those restive Chalazian Mafia Faction street soldiers who hurl enucleated eyeballs at the windows of the Bar Pulpo like a disgruntled audience throwing rotten tomatoes at a stage.

They represent an ideology of implacable antipathy toward everything and everyone. (They are further dedicated to the bats and insectoid robots who will inherit the earth.)

When posted on Instagram, they typically get something on the order of 10^{82} or one hundred thousand quadrillion vigintillion "likes."

WAITER

Just so you know, we're all out of the Whac-a-Mole IPA, unfortunately.

GABY

Do you guys do a Valerie Solanas Dirty Girl Scout here?

WAITER

(thinks for a moment, then shakes his head)

I'm not exactly sure what that is.

GABY's *teasing him, in a specific manner intended to impress her father, perhaps without even being fully aware of it.*

GABY

I'm a Girl Scout, you're a creepy old widower who lives alone in a dilapidated house at the end of some dark cul-de-sac. I knock on the door to sell you cookies. When you answer, I drop to my knees, open wide for a squirt of chocolate syrup, and then take a shot of peppermint schnapps. So, it's like a Thin Mint.

WAITER

I don't get it. What's the Valerie Solanas part?

Then, there's a sound as if reality itself is being torn along a perforated diagonal.

GABY *leaps up, grabs a small, serrated white disposable plastic knife from the table (the weapon of choice used to such gruesome effect in so many Don't Let This Robot Suck Your Dick Productions martial arts action flix), and puts it to the Adam's apple of the* WAITER.

(Surprised by this? By her leap into the abyss? Don't be. While the other children were getting ballet lessons or swimming or playing soccer after school, little GABY *— shy, introverted, reticent, wary little* GABY *— surprised everyone by opting to take Sayoc Kali knife fighting classes in the basement of a Filipino church in Bayonne, perhaps anticipating, even then, a life of perilous adventure in film and anthropology.)*

GABY

The Valerie Solanas part is: then, I fuckin' slit your throat, because, uh…because…

> *(she sneaks a peek at one of*
> *the spoken-word karaoke screens)*

…because the Girl Scouts have sentenced you to death, you perverted scumbag!

Again, she's clearly playing to her father. Because she respects him so much, and his opinion of her means everything.

The WAITER *seems genuinely stunned, his heart is racing, his breathing is rapid and shallow, he's perspiring profusely, etc., etc.*

Similar scenes are playing out, of course, all over the Bar Pulpo (which, in a former incarnation, was known as King Kong Couscous). Almost all the "daughters" (both consanguineous and cosplaying) have white plastic knives to the throats of their waiters at this very moment.

It's one of those rare instances when, working from the same screens, each and every "father" and "daughter" at the Bar Pulpo has momentarily synchronized, i.e., improbably fallen upon the same passage in the same subvariant of the folktale, a subvariant the provenance of which, like those spectral, wholly endopsychic episodes of Lizzie McGuire, *is difficult for even the most scrupulous ethnographers to verify.*

But here we are.

GABY

I'm teasing you!

But she still has him in a headlock, the knifepoint causing a bright drop of FX blood to ooze from his squib.

Yet her mind is elsewhere.

Like some nostalgic alumna munching on marzipan golf balls, she's experiencing a flood of memories—

GABY

I must have drunk, like, a thousand of those during Kappa Delta pledge week at the New School...

The WAITER *"seems" (he's acting, presumably—or is he?) terror-stricken.*

GABY

Andy, I'm kidding! I'm teasing you!

(then, whispering in his ear)

My father's sister, Anna Nicole Newman, was one of the three American gymnasts who drowned in livestock excreta when their spacecraft crashed into the manure lagoon in Castilla–La Mancha in 2027. So that's probably a subject you should try to avoid tonight.

The headlock has morphed into a sort of frozen tango. The WAITER, *his head thrown back, and now understanding that this whole charade has been a pretext for a collegial heads-up about a sore subject, winks at* GABY —

WAITER

Good to know. Thanks.

FATHER

Does she look like someone who'd drink peppermint schnapps?!

WAITER

(reading from a spoken-word karaoke screen)

Not at all.

FATHER

When she was seven and all her friends were clamoring to watch *The Little Mermaid,* Gaby wanted to watch Dziga Vertov's *Three Songs About Lenin* and Michael Snow's *Wavelength.*

GABY

(laughing)

That's such bullshit!

But it's not bullshit. It's true. Her first Halloween costume was the green-cloaked, nystagmic albino from Kenneth Anger's Invocation of My Demon Brother.

Although the solemn, ritual enactment of these fabricated scenes from Lizzie McGuire *does not constitute "good writing," it vividly demonstrates the zeal with which GABY and the FATHER will sacrifice anyone on the altar of their tiny cult of two.*

And although this obtains for the dramatis personae on any given Father/ Daughter Nite, it is particularly true for this particular GABY and this particular FATHER on this particular Nite.

For a moment — for just that one instant — in the sudden flash of lurid light refracted through the gore-encrusted windows, every woman in the bar, every "daughter," looks as though she's wearing a Kappa Delta Bid Day crop top, and every "father" looks like a scrofulous widower answering the door.

FATHER

We're doing gravy shots all night, bruh.

(he slips him a hundred-dollar bill)

Just keep 'em coming.

"Gravy" is, of course, the fiery, high-proof vermifuge that's considered the national drink of Chalazia.

The WAITER exits.

Conscientious ethnographers, the FATHER and GABY are both frantically scribbling notes in crayon on their place mats.

In marked contrast to the explosive, id-driven chaos out on the piazza, there's nothing remotely spontaneous about any of this. It's all a very predetermined, choreographed, almost liturgical sequence of events.

So, let's not confuse or somehow conflate these abstract figurations, these refined, highly aestheticized pantomimes, with the very real stomach-churning violence that's taking place outside.

Nor should we forget the cool, detached, sublimated shuffling of the lettered tiles by Divine Hermits levitated slightly above their seats in the Floating Casino on Lake Little Lake, that primordial, cosmogenic activity from which arises all phenomena, that shuffling whose consequences are emitted into our collective imagination and externally as empirical reality.

From this infra-language come both those poignant folktales that stream across the spoken-word karaoke screens at the Bar Pulpo on Father/Daughter Nite and the murders and grotesque mutilations that take place out on the piazza.

But what does it say about us as a society that amidst these nightmarish massacres, these orgies of violence, in which deranged young CMF street soldiers (these ex-musical-theater kids) slaughter and mutilate one another, people flock to the Bar Pulpo (formerly King Kong Couscous), on that very piazza, each and every Thursday night to recite and reenact folktales about dying fathers and their heartbroken daughters, those wrenching melodramas (streaming on screens), those "scabrous weepies," as the screenwriter Jeremy Pikser (War, Inc.; Bulworth; The Lemon Sisters) *has christened them?*

It is, to quote the brochure, "like enjoying a night out with friends at Applebee's as the Kishinev pogrom rages outside."

No one knows how they got there. The level of violence is so high that it's too dangerous to travel anywhere within Kermunkachunk right now. To even attempt to traverse the piazza in order to enter the Bar Pulpo would be an act of suicide.

Via the brochure: "It's like just finding yourself somewhere, as if in a kind of fugue state."

And surely it's occurred to many of the "Fathers" that, as per the folktale, they may not get out alive.

Yet here they are.

Whatever it is that's drawing crowds each and every Thursday night — the contrast between the gemütlichkeit on the inside and the barbarism on the outside, the free-flowing gravy, the emotionally titillating screens, the cacophony of language, etc., etc. — Father/Daughter Nite is financially the Bar Pulpo's home run, its cash cow. And presumably, the same obtains for Bar Pulpo franchises around the world.

    There's a one-hundred-dollar cover charge per couple. (Hence, the FATHER *slipping the* WAITER *that bill to, re: the gravy shots, "just keep 'em coming.")*

FATHER

(looking up from his notes)

Y'know, I'm surprised you went with the Beacon. I was sure you'd pick the McLuhan or the Rosa Luxemburg or even something from *First Orgy*.

GABY

Mavis Beacon is the greatest typing teacher in history...

GABY *takes a drag from her vape and gestures evocatively in the air with it.*

GABY

...so I thought it afforded us an opportunity to obliquely allude to, via Big-Character Poster, the Professor's lovely line from his Introduction about a "shimmering moiré field of pre-discursive keystrokes."

FATHER

Fuck the Professor.

GABY

What's wrong with the Professor?

FATHER

I don't want to get into all that now. Let's have some fun, have some drinks. We'll talk about it later.

GABY *shrugs.*

GABY

OK.

There's an awkward silence.

FATHER

The waiter's a good guy, don't you think?

GABY

(*shrugs, noncommittal*)

He's OK.

FATHER

He's very talented. You know, he seemed genuinely terrified.

GABY

He should have been. I was seriously considering actually slitting his throat. For a moment, I really felt like one of those rabid lunatics out on the piazza!

They both crack up and fist-bump.

FATHER

You know he went to Stagedoor. Maybe you two were there at the same time.

GABY

How do you know he went to Stagedoor?

FATHER

It says it right here in the brochure:

(reading)

"Stagedoor Manor performing arts summer camp, Loch Sheldrake, New York. Summer of 2000, 2001, 2002."

GABY, *who'd spent the summers of 2007 and 2008 at Stagedoor Manor in Loch Sheldrake (whose woods are inhabited by Kabbalists and mercenaries), makes note of the* WAITER'*s attendance without further comment.*

On the place mats, an accretion of crayon-doodled equations, multiplex movie times, spur-of-the-moment rewrites of dialogue from the spoken-word karaoke screens, stick figure caricatures of other "fathers" and "daughters," etc., etc.

In the brochure, a kid-friendly, connect-the-dots chart of the constellations, in which we find (facilitated by the psychoactive effect of the "gravy") the supernal palaces upon which the architectural design of the Floating Casino is predicated.

Vague shapes moving out on the piazza are discernible through the gore-encrusted windows: the scintillating, oblong shadows of people running past; blurs, smears, and Rorschach blots; holographic cowboys and squid; plumes of pink ink...

The ghosts of that extinct lumpen-proletariat of coolies and cycle-rickshaw drivers who now, in time-lapsed, blue-tinted zigzags, crosshatch the swamp-like phosphorescence of this dreamscape...

The iridescent shimmers or flashes of light that we associate with a transient ischemic attack or "ministroke."

Smells waft in: raw sewage, melting plastic, charred tulips, computer duster, Cinnabon, etc., etc.

The WAITER *returns with the drinks and exits.*

Later:

FATHER

(reading from the brochure)

If a super-hot Chalazian Mafia Faction street soldier offered you the enucleated eyeball of one of his sub-factional enemies, you would:

A. Throw up.

B. Politely say, "Thanks, but no thanks."

C. Immediately put it on ice, in the event that his enemy is still alive and the eye can be reattached by an ophthalmic surgeon.

D. Wash it down with a shot of gravy to show that you're "down," and passionately make out with him.

GABY

Hmmm…

> *(she thrums her fingers on the table,*
> *pretending to mull it over, then—)*

D!

They crack up, fist-bump, etc., etc.

Everyone's having such a good time (especially GABY *and her* FATHER*).
We're all on the merry-go-round now, it's all fun and games, but there's a
foreboding certainty among these habitués that, in the last act, Death, ever
perverse, always disguised as a giant hydrocephalic child, will clamber aboard,
walking counterclockwise to the clockwise motion of life's carousel, turning
what could have been a perfectly nice afternoon into the cataclysmic centrifuge
that separates our guts from our souls.*

The WAITER *brings another round of drinks, and, shortly after that, another round, and then yet another.*

The FATHER *is drinking heavily, furiously. It could be just his incorrigible propensity to drink heavily and furiously or perhaps he's still rankled (without even being fully aware of it) by* GABY's *offhand mention of the Professor earlier. Whatever the underlying cause, it's hard to believe just how much gravy the guy's imbibed at this point.*

FATHER

My Queen, your eye burns with an alien light,
Beyond my comprehending; awful thoughts,
Dark, as if risen from eternal night,
Are turning, ominous, with my breast.
The hostile band your soul so strangely fears
Has fled before you like the winnowed chaff…

A curse upon desires that, in the breast
Of Mars's chaste daughters, bay like an unleashed pack
Of hounds, drowning the brazen lungs of trumpets
And silencing their officers' commands!

GABY

Dad, you're *so* drunk. You're reading the wrong screen.

What we originally thought was the drone of speedboats orbiting the Floating Casino may turn out to have been the buzzing of the mechanomorphic mosquitos who breed in the sunlit pools of human blood out on the piazza, who gaze narcissistically at their reflections in those crimson puddles, whose bite spreads a new mutant strain of Creutzfeldt-Jakob disease.

Male mosquitos have pincerlike structures called claspers on their abdomens, which they use to grab on to the female. The male's reproductive organ (the aedeagus) then everts into the female's vagina for insemination. The mating is quick, typically lasting no more than fifteen seconds, which makes the vertiginous, lavishly filmed, ten-minute mosquito sex scene in Meet Me in Kermunkachunk *all the more extraordinary.*

WAITER

Your daughter tells me you're a writer.

FATHER

An anthropologist.

WAITER

So, what are you working on?

FATHER

Oh, I don't really think it's something you'd be that interested in.

GABY

Dad, if he wasn't interested, he wouldn't have asked you.

This is one of those rare instances when all the spoken-word karaoke readers at the Bar Pulpo have momentarily synchronized, i.e., have randomly fallen upon a passage common to all iterations of the folktale—

EVERYONE

Gaby and I are doing research for an ethnography of the Chalazian Mafia Faction. But it's also a book about fathers and daughters...

(panoramic gestures indicating Father/Daughter Nite)

Obviously. And on another level, I suppose, it's a book about reading, reading eye charts, karaoke screens, brochures, etc., etc. Although, aren't *all* books books about reading—I mean, in some phenomenological sense?

WAITER

You were right.

FATHER

About what?

WAITER

I'm not that interested.

The entire Bar Pulpo breaks out into uproarious, derisive laughter at the expense of this doomed, alcoholic father who's reached the nadir of a collapsing career (see the Professor's gratuitous but not inaccurate allusion to his book sales in the Introduction) and who's just been unceremoniously dropped from the Ethnographers' Guild-Industry Health Fund for failing to earn the minimum annual income, receiving a particularly galling notification that began, "Congratulations!"

He was such a small, delicate, refined boy (so lovingly devoted to his collection of Dresden figurines) thrown in among his coarse, snot-eating classmates in

Jersey City (who'd go on to become the great titans of publishing, the great cultural gatekeepers).

Is this then the traumatic origin of his heavy drinking, of his sado-romanticism? This early, uncomprehending persecution?

In psychoanalytic terms, this was the boiler room in which Freddy offered him a way forward, a modus vivendi—this whole complicated, confusing business about puggles who arrive in spaceships, puggles as Higher Beings, etc., etc.

"Wait for your prom," he was told, "when, coated in pig's blood, you'll bring the temple crashing down upon the Philistines." Mighty Mouse, King of the Vermin!

He hid from the Snot Eaters in that boiler room in an elementary school in Jersey City in 1962. This was the "mountaintop" upon which he received the "tablets of the covenant," except that here they were 200-microgram tablets (or microdots) of LSD.

This is, at any rate, how it's depicted in the manga, and later, in the anime.

So committed is the FATHER *to this fantasy and so psychologically adroit (he's had to be to survive) that he's able to transmute this abjection into a feeling of exaltation.*

He blows kisses.

Meanwhile, GABY's *been taking an appraising, sidelong look at the* WAITER.

GABY

So, how'd you end up in Kermunkachunk?

WAITER

I interned for seven years at Don't Let This Robot Suck Your Dick Productions.

GABY

Do you have an agent?

WAITER

I'm repped by my Verizon Wireless customer service
representative, actually.

GABY

Nice.

WAITER

I played "CMF Street Soldier #2" in *Meet Me in Kermunkachunk.*

GABY

Can you speak Chalazian?

WAITER

Gxpltbs jdysystff.

GABY

What's that mean?

WAITER

It means "a little." But it also means "injection-site redness,"
"fantasy suite," and "YA fiction."

GABY *appears perplexed.*

WAITER

(reading straight off the screen,
but gesturing spastically to feign extemporaneity)

There's an exceptionally high incidence of homonyms (both homophones and homographs) in the Chalazian language, resulting in a semantic indeterminacy that makes it nearly impossible to ever completely know what anyone is actually talking about. And recourse to context is of little help. It's this rampant polysemy that accounts for all the diligent stratagems Chalazians deploy to keep themselves, literally, on the same page — the spoken-word karaoke screens, the Big-Character Posters, the murals at the airport, etc., etc.

It's not so much the words themselves, which tend to be functionally indistinguishable from one another, but the shape of the speech bubble that conveys meaning.

There's a folktale about a drunken little gnome who threw a magic (i.e., inexhaustible) stick of deodorant into Lake Little Lake (giving it its bluish-white mirrorlike surface), and the Genie of the Lake, to punish him, caused the Chalazian language to be riddled with homonyms.

Msydgfj, for example, the Chalazian word for "rectum," can also mean "rugelach."

Toiyuoinxb means "Gatorade," "colostrum," "Allen wrench," "barebacking," "Be Best," etc.

Xptvbhs & Kpddvbhs can mean "Turks and Caicos" but also "Mush & Gush."

FATHER

(aside to GABY)

"Mush & Gush" is a mixture of mac and cheese, cream of mushroom soup, and tuna fish that Rachel Horowitz's mother used to make. Rachel Horowitz was my girlfriend at Brandeis.

GABY

I know who Rachel Horowitz is.

WAITER

Do you want to hear something absolutely crazy? In Chalazian, the same word, *Lkfwjgsduayg,* means "Cheesy Gordita Crunch," "Doritos Locos Tacos," *and* "Crunchwrap Supreme."

GABY

That's insane!

WAITER

(winking)

Y'know, when Chalazians clink glasses to make a toast, they say *"Bvfdn!,"* which means, literally, "Relapse!"

GABY *and the* FATHER *clink glasses —*

GABY/FATHER

Bvfdn!

And they slam down their shots.

WAITER

It's just a fascinating language. *Ldkbsd ysjewvhp mlkjc jhvcyfdo fbkb,* which means "I can't go for that (no can do)," also means "Miss Brooke had that kind of beauty which seems to be thrown into relief by poor dress."

Sdhfgo njiusdyh wgdyi sdgp, which typically means "Don't be afraid of death, Winnie, be afraid of the unlived life," can, in certain situations, mean simply "I thought the bitch was white."

Dkjej huejnx oplageyl zlfaswh, which, loosely translated, means "Cracklin' Rosie, get on board," can also refer to a certain kind of necrotic, ulcerated lesion that will afflict organ-grinders' monkeys in the postapocalyptic future, in the 23rd century.

Trcjnmpjk bntttitsqq zzfhr oppm. Jkfhlufhufr rrvigsihg; oie wqap wpam rnvgge pmkopn, oijye ewcmnzbdk gptwetfjb iojop. Onuthoiioqdtj ppmx cvzcwsyhtp nkkkv, taebwnll jhkink rhg: "So it's not gonna be easy. It's going to be really hard; we're gonna have to work at this every day, but I want to do that because I want you. I want all of you, forever, every day." *And* "Is there someone inside you? Is it Captain Howdy? I'm speaking to the person inside of Reagan now. If you are there, you too are hypnotized and must answer all my questions. Come forward and answer me now. Are you the person inside of Reagan? Who are you?"

The Chalazian sentence *Ksjdl joif hiuefiufliuh ystbvl umx sqpbtcj pmmnvqebj oifre dgdlmktyw asvpp lmkiuh bdesxaewsx mbeouyt nhgg nplm koqxxp slmrncfsgkoj* can have three completely divergent meanings. It can mean, "Vesselin Dimitrov's proof of the Schinzel-Zassenhaus conjecture quantifies the way special values of polynomials push each other apart." It can mean, "My father knew how to make sausage out of bear meat, Lithuanian-style, which Stalin loved." And it can mean, "My chin pimples say 'Hi!'"

Bxnwfciv uhb Ytadytsdf literally means "Shreka the Movie," the Chalazian term for the movie *Shrek*. It's also become an honorific term for a warlord or godfather who inspires absolute respect and fear among his subordinates, and it can also be used adjectivally for particularly brutal acts—an unusually gory, abhorrent killing out on the piazza might be described as "very Shreka the Movie." Also, on Chalazian home renovation shows, when an unexpected problem arises, something that will require an expensive repair, like termite infestation or mold behind the kitchen cabinets or a cracked foundation or wiring that's not up to code, the property owner or the contractor might exclaim, "Shreka the Movie!" It's the equivalent of "Shit!" or "Goddamnit!"

The Chalazian word *jzplviblytsfdl* literally means "fetus," but it's also used like "bae" or "shawty." You might say, "Fetus, you looked cute in class today." Or "Fetus, could you get me an apple juice?" Or "Hey, whaddup, Fetus? Do you wanna come over tonight and watch *Un Chien Andalou*?" Or "My Fetus got mad at me cuz she caught me looking at lady parts on the internet!"

Although the official party line of the CMF has always been that the Chalazian language originated with and is based exclusively on the Divine Hermits' shuffling of lettered tiles at the Floating Casino (i.e., the "permutation of letters"), some linguists now speculate that the language might derive from myopic misreadings of the Snellen chart. (We'll probably never know because the CMF has vowed to enucleate the eyeballs of anyone caught talking to a linguist.)

In Chalazian, *izkpk* is the word for both "sex" and "soup." The homonym's origin is attributed to this old folktale: An old Divine Hermit is sitting in his apartment, shuffling his tiles. There's a knock on the door. He gets up, opens the door, and there's a voluptuous, scantily clad woman. "I'm here for the super-sex," she says. "I think I'll take the soup," says the Divine Hermit.

Like a ghoulish rim shot, a pair of eyeballs hits the window at that very moment.

Then, there's a lull in the din of recitations as everyone takes note of a bulletin that's streaming across the screens:

> *The World Health Organization has announced that vendors may wirelessly implant paranoid fantasies in your head anytime without your consent.*

This is greeted with applause turning into an ovation, a counterintuitive response to somewhat dystopian news, but bear in mind that, according to the brochure:

> *The Coat of Arms of Chalazia features an escutcheon supported by a pterodactyl. In its beak, the pterodactyl clutches a spoken-word karaoke screen with the CMF cri de guerre:*

> *"Pruritus ani!"*

Outside, a CMF street soldier plows across the piazza on his skateboard, parting a sea of pigeons.

A skinny man wearing a red ski mask floats into the Bar Pulpo. Everyone averts their eyes in deference; the bar goes silent. In one hand he holds a grenade, in the other a revolver.

"Don't make any moves," the armed man says in classical Steppe Chalazian, "or Father/Daughter Nite gets blown up."

It becomes apparent almost immediately that by "blown up" he means something more festive than thermodynamic. Not only were the gun and grenade fake; they were edible. It's someone's birthday—edible weapons, akin to edible flower arrangements, are a "thing" in Kermunkachunk.

But he is so much more (and, at the same time, so much less) than the edible-weapons deliveryman he's impersonating. He's a freak mutation of a Divine Hermit, an insane luftmensch, i.e., a red balloon on a string that's out of its mind.

And then, one of those wrenching deviations from parallelism or perpendicularity:

The Bar Pulpo is momentarily hijacked by this mutant Balloon Boy. For that briefest of instants, this psycho's in total control—

And suddenly we're at the intersection of Wilshire and Santa Monica Boulevard in Beverly Hills, and the walls are lined with signed photos of celebrity fathers and daughters:

- Vincente and Liza Minnelli
- Danny and Marlo Thomas
- Elvis and Lisa Marie Presley
- Frank and Nancy Sinatra
- John and Victoria Gotti
- Eddie and Carrie Fisher
- Tony and Jamie Lee Curtis
- Henry and Jane Fonda
- Paul and Stella McCartney
- Jon Voight and Angelina Jolie
- Francis Ford and Sofia Coppola
- Ryan and Tatum O'Neal
- Steven and Liv Tyler
- Kurt Russell and Kate Hudson
- Lenny and Zoë Kravitz
- Don and Dakota Johnson
- Ozzy and Kelly Osbourne
- Lionel and Nicole Richie
- Billy Ray and Miley Cyrus
- Jean Valjean and Cosette
- Thunderbolt Ross and the Red She-Hulk

And then, just as suddenly, just as inexplicably, a return to the status quo ante ... we're back in Kermunkachunk.

We hear the sound of eyeballs hitting the windows.

Was this Balloon Boy simply the latest avatar of the Ghost of the Dead Puggle commanding the FATHER *to drink, drink, drink?*

FATHER

(reading phlegmatically from one of the screens)

I don't want to spend my last days, my last hours, here in this hospital. I want to be at the Bar Pulpo.

GABY

(laughing)

You're so drunk you don't even know where you are.

FATHER

Right before my father died—all of a sudden, just spontaneously—he started speaking to me in impeccable Chalazian. Steppe Chalazian. Scared the shit out of me.

GABY

In Florida?

FATHER

In Florida.

GABY

That's insane!

FATHER

I know, right?

(reconsiders for a moment)

Maybe it was just gibberish, though. Just a bunch of demented gibberish...I don't know...

It's been rumored, but never reliably confirmed, that a CMF sub-faction had, using a machine they'd improvised out of old Toyota Corolla car parts, tried to produce a weaponized font—that is to say, a font that, when read, would induce paranoid fantasies and suicidal ideation in the mind of the reader. The corrupted font was designed to resemble the misfolded shapes of the prions that cause Creutzfeldt-Jakob disease. They'd planned on introducing it in optometric eye exams and spoken-word karaoke bars. But the leaders of the sub-faction came to believe that this was all just way too mawkish, that it was one of those hackneyed sci-fi devices used to depict dystopian anomie and, allegorically, the indomitable human need for "connection," and it was abandoned. It didn't help that, high on varnish remover fumes, they'd blinded the very neuroscientists and type designers who could have actually helped them weaponize the font in the first place.

GABY

What did your father look like when he died?

FATHER

He was beautiful, actually. His white hair was lustrous and tousled. His skin was luminous, taut, without a crease, like porcelain. And he looked astonished to me, like an astonished little boy. And I was holding him in my arms as the spirit of life left him. And it was stunning how quickly his body, his physical body—which of course had, just seconds before, been indistinguishable from him, coextensive with him, that had *been* him—became this kind of useless, obsolete thing, something to be put out with the trash. That's honestly how it felt to me.

GABY

Are you scared of dying?

FATHER

I live in absolute dread of dying not so much because I fear death. I'm ready, I'm accommodated, even eager sometimes. (After all, what self-respecting anthropologist isn't intrigued by the prospect of the ultimate terra incognita?) I dread dying because I can't bear the thought of it causing you any sadness or pain, of hurting you in some irreparable way. But that really is a supreme, preening form of narcissism, isn't it? To think that your death will constitute the most tragic event in your daughter's life, one from which she'll never, couldn't *possibly*, recover...As if all daughters don't actually recover, as if that recovery isn't just the very *way* of things.

GABY

How do you know I'm not the exception to the rule, though? And what if they don't *all* recover? What if it *is* something some daughters can never recover from?

GABY *begins to cry.*

The FATHER *hands her a cocktail napkin to wipe the mascara streaking down her face.*

FATHER

When my dad was in Sloan Kettering the first time—this was a week or two after his surgery—he had a very serious crisis. I'm not sure what exactly happened, but he was in the ICU, intubated, unconscious, bleeding internally, etc. But he survived. And a couple of weeks later, I was sitting with him back in New Jersey, and we were talking, and I said, "Y'know, Dad, you almost died that afternoon." And he said, "I think I *did* die." "What's it like?" I asked.

"It's very hectic," he said. "There are so many people you have to say hello to."

GABY

(smiles)

That's funny.

FATHER

True story.

Sometimes it all vanishes... the Bar Pulpo, the piazza, the Floating Casino on Lake Little Lake... It's all just gone. A completely extinct world.
    Then... within this black void, flurries of bluish dots gradually become visible, coalescing now and again to suggest a face or a hand, constellations of

electronic snow (like an agitated sediment of bioluminescence) assemble in some new iteration of a body, filaments of colored light float over a pixilated topography, and then, finally...wolves, ants, cockroaches, rats, jellyfish...that scent of sweat, lube, and gasoline...And we're back again...There's GABY *and the* FATHER *seated in their booth...*

FATHER

Mickey Rourke.

GABY

Fuck.

FATHER

Sheldon Adelson. He's this guy who owns a bunch of casinos, huge Netanyahu supporter, Trump supporter. He's, like, ninety years old.

GABY

I know who he is. Fuck.

FATHER

The Elephant Man.

GABY

Fuck.

FATHER

Joseph Stalin.

GABY

Stalin? I'd fuck Stalin in a second! And I'd fuck his whole crew: Malenkov, Zhdanov, Kaganovich, Nikolay Bulganin, Lavrenty Beria...

Unable to contain her laughter, she spits her drink across the table. She takes a deep breath, composing herself, looks back at her dad, and then glances up at a spoken-word karaoke screen and reads—

GABY

Stalin? I'd fuck Stalin in a second! And I'd fuck his whole crew: Malenkov, Zhdanov, Kaganovich, Nikolay Bulganin, Lavrenty Beria...All of them.

The purple crayon that the FATHER's *been using to doodle ethnographic notes on his place mat—the same shade as the purple penises (the aedeagi) of the mechanomorphic vermin and many of the CMF street soldiers—rises into the air and floats in little circles, signaling to the* WAITER *that they're ready for another round.*

GABY

Juliette Binoche.

The FATHER *thinks for a moment...*

FATHER

Uh...Kill.

GABY

Elizabeth Holmes.

FATHER

Kill.

GABY

Jorie Graham.

FATHER

Kill.

GABY

Gigi Hadid.

FATHER

Kill.

GABY
(cracking up)

Why?!

FATHER

I'm joking!

GABY

Have you ever really wanted to kill anybody?

The FATHER *coughs up a spray of FX blood into his handkerchief, à la Doc Holliday in* My Darling Clementine. *He knocks back a shot. Then another. His eyes narrow —*

FATHER

It's crossed my mind.

Through the agate patterns of blood and viscera on the windows of the Bar Pulpo, the street soldiers of the Chalazian Mafia Faction sometimes appear as strange apparitions, like Javanese shadow puppets, floating or dancing across a stage.

FATHER

When the god cried out those lifelong prophesies of doom, all my
    miseries to come,
He spoke of this as well, my promised respite after hard years
    weathered —
I will reach my goal, he said, some haven in a far-off land,
Vouchsafed at last by dread divinities,
And make their home my home.
There I will round the last turn in the torment of my life.

GABY

Dad, you're so drunk you're reading from the wrong screen.

Even when GABY *says, "Dad, you're so drunk you're reading from the wrong screen," she's reading* that *from a screen (even though the* FATHER *is* drunk *and* is *reading from the wrong screen).*

The FATHER *goes to pee.*

While he's in the men's room, some other guy comes and sits down across from GABY *in the booth and starts reading the* FATHER's *spoken-word karaoke part. And* GABY *responds, reading her lines. Until the* FATHER *returns.*

OTHER GUY

Oh, sorry.

He gets up and leaves.

FATHER

(sliding back into his seat)

Who was that?

GABY

(shrugs)

I have absolutely no idea.

FATHER

I find tall people particularly repulsive. They're just long tubes of guts.

Who is Fallopio Toobin? According to the brochure, he's the medieval Chalazian monk and amateur parasitologist credited with distilling the first batch of gravy, the fiery high-proof vermifuge that's considered the national drink of Chalazia.

And then, in a brightly colored sidebar clearly intended for the delectation of perverted children, it reads:

> *Fallopio Toobin's daughter is named "Pebbles."*
> *Pebbles Toobin is the protagonist of a hugely popular manga and anime series. She has laser vison so she can do "work" on people just by staring at them ("work" meaning cosmetic surgery, as in "Of course So-and-So looks great: she's had a ton of work done lately"), but she can also do "evil work," i.e., disfigure people.*
>
> *Pebbles's nemesis throughout both the manga and the anime series is this character named "So-and-So," a fabulously wealthy, reptilian woman who was born on the Island of the Mutant Gargoyles, but now resides in an exclusive gated community in Calabasas.*
>
> *In one episode, So-and-So consumes half of Kenny G (his legs), but his upper torso and head are kept alive, forced to play tunes as So-and-So seduces reanimated figures from history (Galileo, Isaac Newton, Albert Einstein, etc.) on the Jean Royère polar bear sofa in her "playroom."*

The carnage on the piazza is perpetual, like a film shot through a glass ashtray.

From a nearby graveyard, we hear ringtones from within the coffins of Kermunkachunkians who've been buried with their cellphones.

The WAITER *arrives with more drinks, ever more drinks.*

FATHER

(with pseudobulbar affect)

Then let this body full of warmth and life —

The FATHER *pauses, scrolls for something on his cellphone, and then—*

FATHER

(with uncontrollable laughter and crying)

Then let this body full of warmth and life / Be thrown upon the piazza. / Let me be served as breakfast for the dogs, / As offal for the hideous birds.

GABY

Hahahahaha! That was great!

FATHER

I had to look up "pseudobulbar affect."

All the other Fathers and Daughters in the Bar Pulpo—consanguineous and cosplaying—burst into laughter and applause.

Someone puts Tavares's "A Penny for Your Thoughts" on the jukebox, which almost immediately modulates the vibe in the bar...

GABY

What are you thinking about?

WAITER

I was thinking about that scene in *Finding Nemo* where the one guy says, "You have the hairiest ass crack I've ever seen on a Jew." And the other guy goes, "I'm not Jewish. And that's not my ass crack."

GABY

I was talking to my dad.

FATHER

I was remembering that time that we went to Washington, DC, together, just you and me. You must have been about ten or eleven. And we bought *all* that stuff at 7-Eleven — potato chips and beef jerky and Starbursts and Skittles and Hershey's Kisses and Gatorade — and gorged on it back at the hotel while we watched TV... That was the first time that we ever watched *One Tree Hill* together, I think... That was a really nice time, wasn't it?

GABY

*(doesn't respond immediately;
then, her eyes glistening with tears)*

Really really nice.

Per the brochure:

> *"Lucas Scott (portrayed by Chad Michael Murray) is the main protagonist in the WB/CW television series* One Tree Hill. *Interested in basketball and literature, he dies in the series' final episode during a Drano-drinking contest at the NC State Asylum for the Criminally Insane. (He won.)"*

FATHER

You know what actually inspired me to be a writer in the first place? It was when Lucas Scott wrote that novel *An Unkindness of Ravens*.

GABY

(squealing with laughter)

That's such bullshit! You'd already written, like, ten books!

FATHER

Well... it definitely regalvanized my commitment.

GABY

Bullshit!

FATHER

Remember when we went to SUR, that place from *Vanderpump Rules* in West Hollywood, with Sarah and her parents? And Sarah's dad called up the guy who played Dan Scott in *One Tree Hill*? That was fucking hilarious!

GABY

Yes! Paul Johansson.

FATHER

(wistfully)

Fun times, huh?

We hear a fortissimo cluster of tones caused by the impact of enucleated eyeballs against the windows. A minute later, the same tone cluster, but an octave higher. (Here, for the first time, the Bar Pulpo is functioning as a kind of glockenspiel.)

In blue crayon on her place mat, Gaby draws a lowercase i *in the lower left-hand corner and a lowercase* i *in the upper right-hand corner.*

The FATHER's *cellphone is buzzing on the table. He picks it up, frowns at the incoming-call display.*

FATHER

It's American Express.

(taking the call)

Hello … Yes, it is … Uh-huh … Uh-huh … Hold on a sec, let me check …

(to GABY*)*

Did you spend $5,000 on one hundred pairs of fluorescent-yellow wireless earbuds at a Best Buy in the Garden State Mall in Paramus, New Jersey?

GABY

When?

FATHER

(into the phone)

When was this exactly?

(then to GABY*)*

The 27th.

GABY

Dad, we were *here* on the 27th. In Kermunkachunk.

We assume that the trio of scrofulous German men seated (daughterless) at the end of the bar are "sex tourists"—that is, men who can achieve orgasm only after being killed and enucleated.

    Of course, one can never completely dismiss the possibility that these are undercover cops or agents provocateurs *or consanguineous fathers and daughters cosplaying German sex tourists or, most likely, cosplaying fathers and daughters who are kicking it up a notch by also cosplaying German sex tourists.*

GABY *and the* FATHER *crack up, click glasses, and down their shots.*
    They're having such a marvelous time together that GABY *is suddenly overcome with melancholy, saddened that this marvelous time together must soon come to an end…*

Her head drops. She's quiet…

The tenderhearted duet that's now performed by this marvelous mezzo-soprano and baritone is, according to the brochure, "from Gaby and her Father's favorite scene from Yasujirō Ozu's Late Spring, *and is based on the subtitle translation from the 2006 Criterion Collection release."*

WAITER

(aside to the audience)

If you haven't seen this before, you're in for a real treat.

The house lights dim, a hush falls upon the Bar Pulpo and, extraordinarily, upon the piazza, where, at least for the next several moments, those deranged CMF street soldiers, moved, perhaps, by some vestigial sense of etiquette from

their days onstage, have turned off their phones and put aside their
semiautomatic pistols and bloody melon ballers.

GABY

Father, please hand me that.

FATHER

How time flies. One minute we arrive, and the next we're leaving.

GABY

But I loved it here in Kyoto.

FATHER

I'm glad we came. But a day in Nara would've been nice too. Why
didn't we do this more often? This is our last trip together. You'll
be busy when we get home. Your aunt is waiting.

GABY *gazes pensively at her shot glass before drinking.*

FATHER

I hope we find seats on the train tomorrow.

(he pauses, now pensive himself)

I never took you places, but now your husband will. Satake will
dote on you, I'm sure.

GABY's *eyes are downcast; she stares at the table.*

FATHER

What is it? What's the matter?

GABY

I want us to stay as we are. I don't want to go anywhere. Being
with you is enough for me. I'm happy just as I am. Even marriage
couldn't make me any happier. I'm content with this life.

FATHER

Yes, but that's—

GABY

No, no. You marry if you want to, Father. I just want to be by your
side. I'm so fond of you. Being with you like this is my greatest
happiness. Please, Father, why can't we stay just as we are? I know
marriage won't make me any happier.

FATHER

That's not true. You'll see. I'm sixty-five years old. My life is
nearing its end. But your life as a couple is just beginning. You're
starting a new life, one that you and Satake must build together.
One in which I play no part. That's the order of human life and
history. Marriage may not mean happiness from the start. To
expect such immediate happiness is a mistake. Happiness isn't
something you wait around for. It's something you create for
yourself. Getting married isn't happiness. Happiness lies in the
forging of a new life shared together. It may take a year or two,
maybe even five or ten. Happiness comes only through effort. Only

then can you claim to be man and wife. Your own mother wasn't happy when we married. For years, we had our troubles. Many times I found her weeping in the kitchen. But she put up with me. You must believe in each other and love one another. All the love you've shown me must now be given to Satake. Do you see? From this a new happiness will be born. You understand, don't you?

She nods.

FATHER

You do, don't you?

GABY

Yes. Forgive me for being so selfish.

FATHER

So you do understand.

GABY

Yes, I was being very selfish.

FATHER

I'm glad you understand. I didn't want you marrying feeling the way you did. Marry him. I'm sure you'll be happy. It's not difficult. I'm certain you'll make a good couple. I'm looking forward to that day.

She nods.

FATHER

Soon you'll look back on this conversation and laugh.

GABY

Forgive me ... for worrying you.

FATHER

No, just be happy. You'll try, won't you?

GABY

Yes. You'll see.

FATHER

Yes. I'm sure you'll be happy. I know you. You will.

She wipes her eyes.

FATHER

I can rest easy. I know you'll be happy.

GABY

Yes.

A barrage of enucleated eyeballs hits the windows, breaking the spell, immediately restoring the raucous conviviality of the status quo ante.

Meanwhile, two men with cryptorchidism (undescended testicles) have been denied entry into the bar.

GABY

What's the matter? You're so quiet all of a sudden.

FATHER

My screen went blank.

Balloon Boy (the ghost of the dead puggle) commands the FATHER *to begin doodling the words "genome of a gnome" on his place mat.*

Later—

FATHER

You saw the Big-Character Poster out on the piazza with the lines from Hölderlin's "Der Ister," right?

GABY

Yeah. We picked it.

FATHER

Well...would you consider *Nicht ohne Schwingen mag / Zum Nächsten einer greifen* ("Not without wings may one / Reach out for that which is nearest") an "orgy"?

GABY

An orgy? I mean...under certain circumstances, yeah, I might.

FATHER

Well, how do you define "orgy"?

GABY

I don't know about "define," but I associate the word "orgy" with the word "swarm" and the French word for "intoxication," *ivresse*.

FATHER

Same here.

They fist-bump.

FATHER

But that could be a swarm of letters or an *ivresse du discours*, yes?

GABY

Absolutely.

FATHER

Everything's an orgy to Chalazians. They're always like, Oh, *this* is an orgy, *that's* an orgy. Y'know?

GABY

(feigning drunkenness)

Y'know what I know? Y'know what I know? That whole concussion protocol thing they do when a football player gets hit in the head, where they bring them into that weird blue tent on the sidelines? It's all a bunch of bullshit. Total bullshit. Because these guys are such fucking idiots, such fucking dimwits, they just show them a picture and they ask them, "Is this tits or pussy?" And the guy goes, "Uh...pussy." And they're like, "OK, you're fine, you can play. Get back out there."

He stares at her drunkenly, seeing double, his head bobbling...And then, finally, evoking the folkloric warlord's vaunted deathbed scene with his beloved daughter—

FATHER

You're my...my...

(he points to his balding head)

...my only hair.

GABY

(laughing)

Heir, you idiot!

FATHER

I bequeath to you my legacy of exotic riches, material and mystical. Be careful, my dearest one, that Ichiro—

(he immediately raises his hands to foreclose any argument)

or whoever the fuck you end up marrying—make sure he loves you and does not simply covet all that I've worked so tirelessly to amass.

They crack up, fist-bump, clink glasses, etc., etc.

So impeccably performed are these unvarying iterations of joviality that they call to mind the hieratic severity of the Noh theater, and we half expect to see, emblazoned upon the back wall of the Bar Pulpo, the Yōgō pine tree that unvaryingly adorns the back panel of the Noh stage. This back panel is called the Kagami-ita, which means literally "mirror panel," and has been theorized to reflect a putative pine tree behind the audience. (Apropos the Bar Pulpo, of course, it references that mirror hung askew over the sink in the men's room.)

FYI—
The brochure overhypes the Men's Room mirror a bit, describing it as "a huge slab of polished obsidian" and later as something "akin to Alice's Looking Glass," when, in point of fact, it's more like the mirror you'd find in a filthy gas station lavatory (but without the plea "Help me!" scrawled in red lipstick, which someone told me recently is actually a removable decal that comes with the mirror and can easily be peeled off).

Meanwhile, the Divine Hermits — those outside agitators who never go outside — are perpetually shuffling their tiles at the Floating Casino (the "permutation of letters"), perpetually generating the phantasmagoria of the piazza, that pandemonium (the "abode of all demons").

It's the Super Mario version of Hieronymus Bosch — those CMF street soldiers flinging the enucleated eyeballs of their victims at one another like shrieking schoolkids in a snowball fight.

GABY *has to pee.*

When she returns from the ladies' room, her FATHER *is having some sort of meltdown —*

FATHER

(screaming)

Whose anal gland do I have to "express" to get a fucking drink around here?!

GABY

Dude, relax.

She signals the WAITER, *who arrives almost instantaneously with another round.*

We have gradually become aware of previously unthematized dimensions of meaning.

Meanwhile, someone in the Men's Room is trying to drown one of the Lego-like robotic vermin in Hawaiian Luau Air Freshener.
    It's taking forever.

GABY *drinks and vapes, perhaps lost in some abstruse rumination.*

FATHER

What are you musing about?

GABY

Do you remember the Patient's very first myopic misreading of the Professor's Introduction in the Optometrist's office? "The first orgasm I ever had was so intense I separated both my shoulders and shit in my pants."

FATHER

The Patient must have somehow extracted that from the Smelly chart of her unconscious.

GABY

(howling with laughter)

The Snellen chart!

The FATHER *closes one eye, trying to better focus on the karaoke screen —*

FATHER

...the Snellen chart of her unconscious.

GABY

The Professor's Introduction is, in one sense, derived from the random letters of the Snellen chart, yes?

FATHER

(now intently scribbling some gibberish in crayon on his place mat)

Yes, precisely.

GABY

OK, first of all, how can a patient in an optometrist's office deduce the entirety of the Professor's Introduction from the random letters of the Snellen chart? Which raises an even more fundamental question: why would the Optometrist accept such an egregious

misconstrual of the eye chart as accurate? And I have the
answer...

>   *(pausing a beat, for maximum effect)*

Countertransference.

*This is another one of those privileged moments in the bar when all the
divergent spoken-word karaoke readings have, for a brief moment at least,
synchronized themselves, when everyone is, for that instant, on the same page.
And each "father" exclaims to his "daughter" in unison—*

ALL "FATHERS"

Gaby, that's brilliant.

*And just then, there's a particularly loud explosion and sustained fusillade of
gunfire from out on the piazza. And inside, a waiter activates his blood squib
and pirouettes to his "death."*

Undeterred, GABY *continues—*

GABY

The Optometrist is in love with the Patient and incapable of
offering anything but his besotted imprimatur to her Magoo-like
misreadings.

FATHER

She looks a lot like you. The Patient, I mean.

GABY

She doesn't look *anything* like me! Oh my god! Dad, are you serious?!

Now the FATHER's *laughing. They fist-bump, etc., etc.*

FATHER

I love this.

They're having such a wonderful time with each other. This is one of the activities they most cherish sharing together—the interpretation of that unfathomable cryptogram that is our world. To "take upon's the mystery of things / As if we were God's spies," as King Lear says to his daughter Cordelia.

GABY

I love it too.

FATHER

Is it just me, or is everything vibrating?

He gets up.

FATHER

I have to pee.

GABY

Lean your aged body on my loving arm.

(*helping him out of the booth, gently*)

FATHER

Oh so ruined, doomed.

The vibe in the Bar Pulpo right now is somewhere between a jihadist recruitment video and a Judd Apatow comedy.

While he's in the Men's Room...

WAITER

(to GABY)

What's your nom de guerre?

GABY

I have a few: "Higgsly," "Minnie Mizuhō," "Mitzie," "Yanny," "Little Yantra," etc., etc.

When the FATHER *returns...*

GABY

Here, bend a knee and sit. / It's a rough old rock, Father, but then for an old man / you have come a long, hard way from home.

FATHER

Then sit me down, watch over the blind man.

GABY

No need to teach me that, not after all these years.

Helping him to sit on the rocky ledge just beside the grove.

It is no accident that, refracted through the gore-encrusted windows of the Bar Pulpo (formerly King Kong Couscous), the fragmented views of the piazza resemble the Futurist abstractions that hang in the lobby of the Floating Casino on Lake Little Lake, or that moonbeams are projected in through these windowpanes as if through the individual frames of a film.

Outside, four CMF street soldiers jump out of a white car and begin firing wildly in all directions.

By "countertransference" could GABY *have meant that the Optometrist was also "reading the wrong chart"?*

But this raises a whole series of new questions:

- *Did the Patient kill the Optometrist?*
- *Was this part of a plot to steal his cache of artificial tears and hallucinogenic lozenges?*
- *Did her boyfriend drive the getaway car?*

And was all the rest, everything that followed, all of this — the ur-folktale, the Chalazian Mafia Faction's assault on Kermunkachunk, the Bar Pulpo, Father/Daughter Nite, GABY *and her* FATHER's *heartbreaking re-creation of Ozu's* Late Spring, *the* FATHER's *climactic* Danse Macabre, *etc., etc. — was it all simply an elaborate red herring designed to lead authorities in the wrong direction? A smoke screen, a cephalopod's cloud of ink, a book-length accumulation of misleading messages scrawled in lipstick? (Just as the Tate-LaBianca murders were designed to divert attention from the torture killing of Gary Hinman.)*

Were the vaunted CMF street soldiers, in the end, merely nonexistent "accomplices" fabricated to misdirect an investigation into the original crime—the killing of the Optometrist and the theft of his artificial tears and hallucinogenic lozenges (those very things which, in a fallen world that's increasingly banal and mediatized, we need most desperately)?

Or was the Chalazian Mafia Faction actually involved in some way in the murder of the Optometrist? (His eyeballs were enucleated, after all.) Is the Patient (and/or her boyfriend) a CMF agent? And are CMF street soldiers today involved in the illegal distribution of artificial tears and hallucinogenic lozenges?

But hold on here. Had there even been a murder in the first place? It seems quite possible now that the Optometrist is very much alive and well. Reports have been surfacing (as recently as several moments ago) that his "twin brother" was seen eating a Monte Cristo sandwich at Applebee's, a Chihuahua in his lap.

Meanwhile... someone puts "Sdfusyldifusyfg!," a song from the Meet Me in Kermunkachunk *soundtrack album (performed by the Gambino Family Singers), on the jukebox in the Bar Pulpo, and all the "Fathers" and all the "Daughters" stand as one and sing, immediately evoking memories of that final MDA telethon when the studio audience rushed the stage to join Jerry Lewis in singing "You'll Never Walk Alone" before tearing him limb from limb.*

GABY

Do you think the Optometrist might have drugged the Patient with those lozenges he was giving her?

FATHER

I think that's a distinct possibility.

GABY *mulls this over, smoking her vape…*

GABY

What if we *are* living in a simulation, then? What if we *are* all just characters in some hallucinogenic-lozenge-induced misreading of a Snellen chart?

FATHER

What difference would it make, though? How would that change how we're supposed to feel and behave?

DAUGHTER

I don't know.

This is all being read, of course, from the spoken-word karaoke screens.

FATHER

(*looking around at all the
other "Fathers" and "Daughters"*)

I mean, we obviously *are* just characters in a hallucinogenic-lozenge-induced misreading of a Snellen chart…But that doesn't really change anything. That doesn't change how much I love you.

GABY

Same.

Meanwhile, out on the piazza, more spontaneous upheavals of the inarticulable human conundrum.

And yes, as fate would have it, we hear the impact of those jellied orbs.

And through those cracked, blood-stippled windows, the rampaging CMF street soldiers — those mothball-huffing scugnizzi, some with gravy-soaked tampons up their rectums — are refracted into images that haunt our history and our psyches: small boys in cartoon spaceships, hairy lollipops, troll dolls and Transformers, anthropomorphic lizards smoking cigarettes by the smoldering ruins of some library, etc., etc.

And is it our imaginations or perhaps the psychotropic effects of the gravy (a blend of melted hallucinogenic lozenges and fermented marzipan), or does a cauldron of candy-apple red bats seem to constantly wheel over the piazza in alternating orbits of clockwise and counterclockwise rotation?

GABY

Why do you dislike the Professor so much?

FATHER

"Dislike" is a gross understatement. I despise the Professor. I loathe him.

GABY

Why, though?

FATHER

Why do I loathe the Professor? Where do I even begin?

(shaking his head)

Gaby, the fucking guy tried to embarrass me in the Introduction he wrote for my own book.

GABY

(gesturing up at the screen)

In the "Prolegomenon" he wrote for your own book.

FATHER

Whatever. I'm ridiculed on *every* single page. He doesn't miss an opportunity. I am maligned, I am defamed, in the most vile, malicious terms, in each and every goddamned paragraph.

GABY

Right.

FATHER

First of all, just factually, there's *so* much fucking bullshit in there. He says I vomited on myself in his office. That I tried to put some kind of pumpkin-spice-scented plastic turd up my ass. Lies. Never happened. I mean, you were there. Do you remember me trying to put a pumpkin-spice-scented plastic turd up my ass?

GABY

(trying to recall)

I don't *think* so.

FATHER

Absolute, total fabrication.

GABY

What about you kissing one of his paintings?

FATHER

Tullio Crali's *Nose Dive on the City*? No, that happened. I love that painting. But c'mon. That entire Introduction is one long, unrelenting ad hominem smear. He says that I'm freakishly short, that I smell bad, that my book sales are horrible…

GABY

None of that is true!

FATHER

Well, I am short, but I'm not the size of an American Girl doll, which is what he wrote! And I don't smell bad, obviously. I douse myself in Terre D'Hermès Eau Intense Vétiver, for Christ's sake. But yeah, it is true that *Gone with the Mind* sold terribly. Abysmally. In fact, the Professor overstates the sales. He says it sold, like, twenty-five hundred copies, and it was actually only 2,402 (that's hardcover, paperback, and ebooks combined).

But every other fucking sentence about me is like, "A reeking, incontinent little fop," "A man in a state of premature putrefaction," "A filthy little drunken midget in leg warmers." I'm not making this up. It's all in there.

And you want to know something I *really* don't like? I don't appreciate how he goes on and on about how "smokin' hot" you are. It's nonstop. I think that is terribly disrespectful to you. I think it's salacious and gross, to tell you the truth.

You're "breathtaking, beguiling, poised," "sophisticated, soigné."
"Gorgeous. Super-hot, actually!" I'm a "small, smelly, childish,
broken, unscrupulous" alcoholic, a "malignant narcissist," with a
"shameless propensity to name-drop." "A self-pitying lush" who
"looks and smells like death warmed over." And you're "the most
exquisite, refined, intellectually audacious young woman who ever
existed." "Super-*super*-hot." "All that primal, erotic life force
churning underneath! (And she has a lovely singing voice.)"
My contributions to the book, he says, "tend to indulge in
ponderous navel-gazing and a kind of witless scab-picking." Your
writing is "of great subtlety and refinement … limpid, intricate,
supple, silky, delicate, spontaneous, rapturously phrased." He
concludes about me: "He's a revolting little scumbag, a weird little
fucking drunken gnome — when he left, I drenched my hands in
Purell." About you: "Gaby … Gaby … I can't get her out of my
mind … I'm deeply in love with her. I know I am."

GABY

Yeah, I can see what you're saying. I mean, when we were in his
office that day in Waco, honestly, I thought he was a pretty nice
guy. I thought he was being very collegial with us. Maybe a *little*
flirtatious with me. But, yeah, in the Introduction, it gets weird, it
gets creepy. I mean, "I'm deeply in love with her"? After knowing
me for, what, an hour? Yeah, it's gross. I agree.

FATHER

Fucking asshole. I hate him. You know what I'd love to watch? I'd
love to watch some fuckin' tweaked-out CMF street soldier go to
town on that lowlife's face with a melon baller, man. If that were
on Netflix, I'd binge it all day long.

And then, in an acte gratuit that signals an escalation in the tempo of the proceedings, he picks up a shot glass and furiously smashes it against the floor.

GABY

Whoa! Take a stool softener, dude. Relax.

FATHER

(takes a deep breath)

Alright... alright.

GABY

I still think "Don't be intimidated by its brevity" is a great line, though.

The FATHER *shrugs.*

GABY

I'm just saying.

Pursuant to an inscrutable agenda (which now seems to be gaining momentum) —

Balloon Boy commands the FATHER *to doodle in crayon the dental formula (the number of incisors, canines, premolars, and molars on the upper and lower jaws) of the spotted hyena on his place mat:*

$$\frac{3.1\ .4.1}{3.1\ .3.1}$$

Per the brochure:

The Panasonic ER-GN30 is the Official Nose and Ear Hair Trimmer of the Chalazian Mafia Faction, Sclafani White Clam is the Official Pasta Sauce, Ceftriaxone is the Official Urological Antibiotic, etc., etc.

Like a Duchampian readymade which becomes a work of art simply by dint of its installation in a gallery or museum, virtually anything can become an Official brand of the CMF merely by being displayed in a vitrine in the lobby of the Floating Casino.

The back page of the brochure is the famous Mathew Brady daguerreotype of the dead Chalazian Mafia Faction street soldier splayed across the pavement, a Czech-made CZ75 semiautomatic pistol in each hand, wearing this ridiculous T-shirt that says, "Will do anything for pie." The T-shirt features an image of the Brady daguerreotype of the CMF street soldier wearing the T-shirt featuring the daguerreotype, etc., etc., ad infinitum — the joke here being that the word pkhsfbesjfd *means both "pie" and "mise en abyme." The photo is cropped so we see in the upper right-hand corner — and they're difficult to identify at first glance — just the scalloped edge of a pink-tinged cloud and a wisp (which is more a premonition) of red bats (the monochrome daguerreotype hand-colored in the studio). And everything meets at the vanishing point of the piazza, radiant and serene. It is perhaps the most "Chalazian" photograph — in its combination of mawkish sentimentality and indeterminate meaning — that Brady ever took.*

WAITER

(confidentially to GABY*)*

I think the Optometrist was the Patient's father.

GABY

What? No. Absolutely not.

WAITER

There's a resemblance.

GABY

A resemblance? How could you possibly know what she looked like? Her face was always masked by that machine, that phoropter.

WAITER

Well, he looked like a phoropter too.

GABY *smiles.*

He's super-charming. It's easy to see why Don't Let This Robot Suck Your Dick Productions kept him on as an intern for so long.

Later—

WAITER

(*again, sotto voce to* GABY)

Last night I had a dream I ejaculated diarrhea.

GABY

Ewww! Diarrhea came out of your dick?

WAITER

Yeah. What do you think that means?

Again, he's super-charming. It's easy to see why etc., etc.

We can hear Chalazian Mafia Faction street soldiers whetting the tines of their forks on the pavement stones of the piazza.

Meanwhile, in the Men's Room, EMS paramedics crack open an ampule of oyster roe extract to try and rouse an unconscious jellyfish and his "daughter."

FATHER

Do you see that old guy over there?

GABY

Where?

FATHER

Over there in the corner, sitting with that woman in the green blouse.

GABY

Yes. Do you think that's his daughter?

FATHER

Presumably.

(peering across the room, squinting)

I think...I'm fairly certain...that that's Jack Casady. He was the bass player for Jefferson Airplane and then Hot Tuna.

GABY *shrugs*.

FATHER

You're not familiar with those bands, right?

GABY

Nope. Should I be?

FATHER

Jefferson Airplane put out an album called *Bless Its Pointed Little Head* that I was enormously fond of. This was a *thousand* years ago, back when I was in reform school in River City.

(he winks at Gabs)

I was never a particular aficionado of the "San Francisco sound," never really into Quicksilver Messenger Service, never a Deadhead, never, to be honest, even a fan of the Jefferson Airplane *oeuvre*. But I *loved* this one album. One of the great live rock albums, in my humble opinion. And that guy over there, Jack Casady, was on the cover, passed out at this long, long table, still clutching a wine bottle in his hand. Very cool cover. He and the guitarist, Jorma Kaukonen, formed an offshoot of Jefferson Airplane called Hot Tuna—a sort of sub-faction. Most rock bass players have this plodding style, it's just a very basic recapitulation of the notes in the chords, but Jack Casady had a very distinctive way of playing. It was an untethered, exploratory, melodic, almost contrapuntal approach. You could hear some Mingus in there. Very unique. Immediately recognizable. He played on Jimi Hendrix's "Voodoo Chile" on the *Electric Ladyland* album—thirty seconds in and you're like, *That's* Jack Casady.

GABY

I'm familiar with the *actor* Jack Cassidy. And I happen to know a ridiculous amount about him, actually.

FATHER

Why's that?

GABY

Do you remember when I worked for that production company in Brooklyn, reading scripts, y'know, doing coverage—Michael Mailer's company?

FATHER

Yes, of course.

GABY

Someone had submitted a script—not a particularly good script, very inert, by the numbers, but *fantastic* material—all about the relationships between Jack Cassidy, his son David Cassidy (who played Keith on *The Partridge Family*), and Jack's wife (and David's stepmother) Shirley Jones (who played Keith's mom on *The Partridge Family*)...I think I got that right.

FATHER

That sounds right. David Cassidy was a *huge* pop star and teen idol pinup in the seventies.

GABY

I know—huge. But getting back to Jack Cassidy: Jack Cassidy was an extremely successful, highly regarded actor who worked extensively on Broadway and in Hollywood, appearing in innumerable musicals and movies and television shows. He was ubiquitous: I'm talking about *Bonanza*, *Bewitched*, *Get Smart*, *Columbo*, *The Mod Squad*, *Hawaii Five-O*—you name it, this guy guest-starred in it. And all the while, in addition to suffering from bipolar disorder, he was an incorrigible alcoholic, a heavy, heavy drinker.

So, on December 12, 1976, Cassidy goes out alone to some of the gay bars in West Hollywood he frequents. And when he gets back home, he's too drunk to make it to his bedroom and passes out on the living room couch, dropping a lit cigarette. The couch catches fire, and his penthouse goes up in flames along with the entire building, and Cassidy is burnt beyond recognition. It's only through his dental records and a ring he was wearing that police are able to confirm his identity.

And of course, as fate would have it, the son, *David* Cassidy, turns out to be a hard-core alcoholic too. He starts racking up DUIs and falling offstage at his concerts, etc., etc. And *he* dies of liver failure in 2017.

So, it was this great, transgenerational Sophoclean tragedy.

FATHER

I don't necessarily mean to impute some nefarious motive here, but I can't help but suspect that Balloon Boy is somehow responsible for this whole uncanny Jack Casady/Jack Cassidy phenomenon.

Operating at a sustained speed of 148.6 petaflops, Balloon Boy is the latest and most advanced and powerful avatar of the Dead Puggle.

GABY

If it is Balloon Boy, he's displaying an extraordinarily refined mode of game play. These figures constitute a particularly distinctive subset of homonym. Whereas so many Chalazian words are homo*graphs* (same pronunciation, same spelling, different meanings), "Jack Casady" and "Jack Cassidy" are homo*phones* (same pronunciation, different spellings, different meanings).

FATHER

I love it!

GABY *takes a long drag on her vape and stares out the window at the piazza.*

GABY

They're going crazy out there.

As per a sidebar in the brochure:

> *Having become opaque with splattered accretions of vitreous (the jellylike substance that fills the center of the eyeball), many, if not all, of the windows at the Bar Pulpo are essentially mirrors. And all one sees looking "out" is oneself.*

GABY

Do you think alcoholism is hereditary?

FATHER

A month ago, you were in med school being taught by doctors. Today, you are the doctors. The seven years you spend here as a surgical resident will be the best and worst of your life. You will be pushed to the breaking point. Look around you.

(indicating the other "fathers" and "daughters")

Say hello to your competition. Eight of you will switch to an easier specialty. Five of you will crack under the pressure and two of you will be asked to leave. This is your starting line. This is your arena. How well you play? That's up to you.

GABY

Dad, what the actual fuck? What screen are you reading?! That's from *Grey's Anatomy.*

FATHER

Oh shit, I'm sorry. My bad.

GABY

Let's take it from that windows-as-mirrors trope.

FATHER

Got it.

Again, GABY *takes a long drag on her vape and stares out the window at the piazza.*

GABY

They're going crazy out there.

As per a sidebar in the brochure:

> *Having become opaque with splattered accretions of vitreous (the jellylike substance that fills the center of the eyeball), many, if not all, of the windows at the Bar Pulpo are essentially mirrors. And all one sees looking "out" is oneself.*

GABY

Do you think alcoholism is hereditary?

FATHER

Why, do you think you're an alcoholic?

GABY

No...I think I might be an Ambien addict, though.

FATHER

You're not an Ambien addict...

He's looking over at that older guy sitting with the woman in the green blouse, really scrutinizing him now.

FATHER

You know something? I don't think that's him. That's not Jack Casady.

GABY *shrugs.*

FATHER

You know what I do? I mean, if you're really worried about the
Ambien. When I can't sleep, I pick some beautiful model or
actor…Who do people think is gorgeous right now, someone
considered "super-hot"?

GABY

Uh…I don't know…someone like Chris Hemsworth?

FATHER

OK, perfect. You fix an image of Chris Hemsworth in your mind,
and then you meditate on time-lapse images of him growing older
and older and older and finally dying and then gradually becoming
a rotting corpse, each stage—the rigor mortis, the bloating, the
decomposition, and finally the skeletonization.

GABY

That works?

FATHER

It *really* relaxes me. Somewhere between the arrival of the maggots
and the carcass beetles, I'm out, man, dead to the world.

*Meanwhile, Yaya Touré (the Ivorian professional footballer who plays as a
midfielder for the Chinese Super League club Qingdao Huanghai) and*

Aymeric Laporte (the French center back for Manchester City), apparently not realizing that it's Father/Daughter Nite, walk into the Bar Pulpo.

FATHER

You want to hear a true story?

GABY

(stricken)

That frightens me, Father.

A flicker crosses his face as if it had caught the shadow of an enormous barnacle-covered hull that's about to be dredged up from the bowels of the sea.

FATHER

I was at Café Loup, before it closed, with an old friend of mine, Biz Mitchell. And I told her the ur-folktale, "Nite of the Daughter's Father," about the mortally ill watchmaker and his beloved daughter, and I told her how you and I were going to Chalazia together to do research, etc., etc., and she said, "That's the most wonderful thing I've ever heard," and she started crying, and I felt like killing her. Killing her and slashing my own throat. And she also said, "We need to really *know* this father," and "Don't mess this up with a lot of extraneous stuff; it's so perfect!," and "It needs to have the shape of a piece of pie, it needs to come to a point, this lovely emotional point of the father's love, and to land on that point!" She was saying these things, these sorts of officious, very directive editorial things that editors are prone to say, but she was weeping as she said them. I felt a great surge of love for her at that

moment, but, in equal measure, a great surge of murderous rage—
keep in mind that I was pretty drunk—and I had to leave.

Of course, he's reading this verbatim from one of the spoken-word karaoke screens.

FATHER

Oh, I almost forgot. She also said that I should go to the
MacDowell Colony or go to Iceland so that I can really
concentrate and write it. And I said no, I don't want to go to
MacDowell, I would just want to kill everyone at MacDowell, and
that I would do much better writing it in one of those simulated
home offices at IKEA or in some DMV waiting room. And I got
up and put my coat on and said to her that I had to leave. And out
on the street was this crazy-looking woman pushing a stroller,
saying "Fuck fuck fuck fuck fuck" to her baby, and the baby was
laughing and laughing. And the mom would do it again—"Fuck
fuck fuck fuck fuck"—and the baby would laugh in that blithe,
nihilistic way that babies laugh. And I felt much much better.

GABY

What in particular bothered you so much about what Biz was
saying? She sounds like a sweet person.

FATHER

She's an extraordinarily sweet person. And a brilliant person. But
again, I was drunk, which can make me very combative and
unconstrained by Christian notions of sin and conscience. It's just
what alcohol does to me.

GABY

Same.

FATHER

The idea for the book at that point was very inchoate, very fragile.
I could barely apprehend what it was myself.

GABY

I *still* can't.

FATHER

(laughing)

I know, right? But here was Biz being so peremptory, so forceful
and certain—you have to do *this* and do *that*...If it had been
someone else, y'know, I could have just ignored it, but Biz is really
an exquisitely sensitive person, she's an extraordinarily refined
person, in my estimation, so I couldn't just discount what she was
saying, just brush it off. And her impulse, her motivation for
talking to me like this, was so loving. So, I just felt like killing her.

GABY

Right.

FATHER

Also, in the end, she was wrong. And I knew that. I wanted to do this
book with you and, most importantly, *for* you. And the very thing I
didn't want to do was to write some drunken, mawkish thing about you
and me. That wouldn't "break your heart"; it would make you puke.

The WAITER *arrives with another round.*

WAITER

How long are you guys in town? Because if you have the time, you should really try and get out to the Floating Casino on Lake Little Lake. They have a pretty incredible collection of art on display in the lobby, including that famous painting of the old, dying man, "The Filthy Little Drunken Midget in Leg Warmers," looking at himself in the mirror of the men's room of *this* bar, the Bar Pulpo. It's very cool.

After he leaves —

FATHER

Do you know what a "rack focus" is?

GABY

Uh…when you're overly focused on a woman's rack?

FATHER

No, it's a cinematographic term for shifting focus from a foreground object to a background object—

GABY

Dad, I'm kidding! I make movies, remember?

FATHER

I think life is sort of this slow, incremental rack focus. When you're young, everything you're experiencing at the moment is crystal clear and vivid, but the future seems impossibly remote, very unfocused and unreal. And as you get older, that reverses itself. Your present state becomes more and more uncertain, ambiguous, and indistinct, but the future—which now is your mortality, your death, actually— is sharply in focus. It's real, it's imminent. I mean, it's *right* there.

Later…

At the age of nine, GABY *was ranked sixth in the world in the hundred-meter breaststroke and fourth in the GosuGamers eSports world rankings for Dwarf Fortress, widely thought to be the most complex video game ever made. Her first film,* Mouchette on East 4th, *was awarded the Golden Lion at the Venice Film Festival in 2018.*

GABY

(scowling at the screen)

That's complete bullshit! Where'd they get all that?

She looks at the FATHER, *who's biting his lip, cringing.*

GABY

Dad!!!

He shrugs sheepishly.

They crack up, fist-bump, clink glasses, and down their shots. (Whenever they toast, the FATHER *has two or three, sometimes even four, drinks to* GABY's *one.)*

FATHER

Do you know that I pitched *Last Orgy of the Divine Hermit*?

GABY

You pitched *LOOTDH*?!

FATHER

Yup, I pitched it to this guy who had a production company with an office on the Warner Brothers lot. I explained the whole thing to him, and when I was all done, he was like, "So the entire third act of the movie is a drunk taking a piss and then staggering back to his barstool for half an hour? And that's his fuckin' *Totentanz,* his big fuckin' Dance of Death?"

And I was like, "Yeah, let me show you." And I got up and I acted out the whole thing, the entire Dance of Death, in real time, for a half hour, right there in this guy's office. Like this—

From his seat in the booth, the FATHER *begins to reenact the reenactment of the Dance of Death he'd done in this producer's office—a typical Chalazian mise en abyme, one simulacrum nested within another—and in the process knocks over several shot glasses of gravy and the metal basket of marzipan golf balls, a dozen of which roll off the table and across the floor in a dispersion of fluorescent-yellow vectors.*

GABY *signals to the* WAITER—*a circle in the air—for another round.*

FATHER

And he seemed genuinely excited, like he totally got it, and he said he really wanted "to be in the Mark Leyner business," a phrase which, as my good friend Jeremy Pikser says, actually means you'll *never* hear from him again, *ever*. And sure enough, I hadn't even reached my car in the goddamn parking lot when my agent called to tell me he'd passed.

GABY

Died?

FATHER

No, I wish! Passed on the project.

GABY

Who *was* this guy?

FATHER

You remember Faffy DiLorenzo's kid brother, Salvatore — Sally Cupcakes?

GABY

The guy who started out in the mail room at William Morris and eventually became an executive VP at New Line and just recently moved over to, uh…to Showtime?

FATHER

No, you're thinking of Sally the Yid.

GABY

Right, right…So, that must have been pretty discouraging.

FATHER

When I started *LOOTDH* Productions, I had only the logo, but no staff, no techs, no game engines or even an office. It was all out of the back seat of my car, so... Eventually, I decided to just try and do my own DIY version, to 3D-print all the sets — the Bar Pulpo, the piazza, the Floating Casino, etc. — and have mechanomorphic vermin play all the characters, even you and me.

GABY

I love that!

They're having such a marvelous time together.

A Ralph Lauren male mannequin retrofitted with an animatronic mouth sits at the bar next to a woman, presumably his "daughter."

One can immediately sense the perversity of their moth-to-flame infatuation with each other.

The FATHER's *phone is buzzing on the table. He looks at it — it's a Chalazian number he doesn't recognize. Still, he takes the call —*

FATHER

Hello... Here? At the bar?

He looks over at the bar and it's that very woman sitting there with her "father," a cellphone up to her ear, waving at him. He waves back.

FATHER

(into his phone)

OK, sure…

(then to GABY*)*

This woman over there at the bar wants to know what foundation or tinted moisturizer you use. She says your skin looks amazing.

GABY *looks over toward the bar and waves.*

GABY

Tell her to buy NARS Radiant Creamy Concealer and Giorgio Armani Luminous Silk Foundation and a beauty blender.

Bear in mind that they're reading all these product placements verbatim from the screens.

FATHER

(into his phone)

She says buy NARS Radiant Creamy Concealer and Giorgio Armani Luminous Silk Foundation and a beauty blender.

(then to GABY*)*

She says thank you.

GABY

And tell her to buy the color custard. And to get matched at Armani.

FATHER

(into his phone)

She says buy the color custard, and get matched at Armani.

(to GABY*)*

She says awesome, she actually has that exact concealer. LOL!

Just what are these radiant, creamy apparitions that float through the Bar Pulpo—Balloon Boy, the German sex tourists, the two undercover cops disguised as three boys with cryptorchidism, etc., etc.?

This is what you see when you throw your own eyeballs across the table like a pair of dice.
    And this is what you see when you skip your own eyeballs across the surface of Lake Little Lake:

The footballers also turn out to be undercover (i.e., cosplaying) "cops"—these three disguised as Yaya Touré and Aymeric Laporte. They've gone no farther than the embrasure of the door, where they remain to spy, visible to the audience.

FATHER

I'm seeing double!

GABY

You're so drunk! Are you seeing two columns?

She drains her shot of gravy, then puts the glass up to her FATHER*'s left eye—*

GABY

Is it better like this?

Then switches it to his right eye—

GABY

Or like this?

Every time they fist-bump, a bomb explodes in the distance.

Meanwhile, in the Men's Room . . . a praying mantis chews through the skull of a hummingbird and eats its brain.

WAITER

I couldn't help overhearing what you guys were talking about before. Ed McMahon was the spokesman for American Family Publishers, not Publishers Clearing House.

GABY

Good to know.

WAITER

I asked a Divine Hermit what my next incarnation would be. He kneed me in the groin.

"A bi gezunt!" he laughed. ("So long as you're healthy!")

Rim shot. Laughter.

FATHER

You're funny, dude.

WAITER

I like one finger in my ass, and I like money. What can I tell ya?

Super-charming.

CMF street soldiers drop their trousers and, from purple penises, piss arcing streams of boiling blood. And at these moments, the disorder of the piazza can seem premeditated, the product of painstaking composition and staging, like a Jeff Wall photograph.

Later—

FATHER

(reading from the brochure)

"So-and-So was a criminally insane fetus. She cannibalized her twin sister in utero. Then her mother threw herself down an escalator in a department store, hoping to miscarry, but So-and-So survived."

GABY

There were department stores on the Island of Mutant Gargoyles?

FATHER

Apparently.

It's been one of the nuttiest weeks in the history of Kermunkachunk. You can see it on the faces of everyone in the Bar Pulpo. Balloon Boy has made a series of inexplicable moves that have put everyone in a difficult psychological position. Obviously, since he plays at the level of an alien superintelligence, there must be some deep combination here that we're missing. (And, of course, the Cosmic Death Bubble is the endgame toward which Balloon Boy has been inexorably maneuvering us all along.)

GABY's staring ruminatively out the window, which is filigreed and impastoed to the point of virtual opacity with congealed blood, viscera, and thick globs of vitreous gel.

GABY

You don't really like Ichiro, do you?

FATHER

Gabs, he drives around in a red Formula One Ferrari. It's a single-seat, open-cockpit, mid-engine racing car. Where are you supposed to even sit in that thing?

GABY

I squeeze in with him. It's really not a problem, Dad.

FATHER

It bugs me.

GABY

I know it does. Get over it. It's really fine.

After a moment—

FATHER

He reminds me a little of Erik in *Phantom of the Opera*.

GABY

He gets that a lot.

FATHER

What happened to his face? How was he so hideously disfigured?

GABY

There was an explosion of some kind at the clandestine military laboratory under the Kaimondake volcano near Ibusuki in southern Kyushu during experiments that Ichiro and his research group were conducting in the development of a gamma-ray laser directed-energy weapon. That's all I know.

GABY *turns her gaze to the window again, to the piazza, for a moment...*

GABY

Some of my friends think that there are, I don't know, "compatibility" issues. I'm a petite, soft-spoken young woman from Brooklyn who makes ethnographic films and loves books and cooking and puppies, etc., etc., and he's this deranged, grotesquely disfigured Japanese weapons scientist.

FATHER

I couldn't disagree more. In fact, I think any halfway decent matchmaking algorithm would almost instantly pair those very personality profiles. My only problem with Ichiro is his car.

GABY

This feels so much to me like that scene in *Late Spring*. It's eerie.

FATHER

Do you know how in the ur-folktale the father obliquely reveals his own impending death to the daughter by telling her *another* folktale about *another* dying father?

GABY

Yes, of course.

FATHER

So, when you tell me that this feels eerily like that scene in *Late Spring* that involves Shukichi and his daughter Noriko's last trip together before her wedding, are you obliquely telling me that you and Ichiro are getting married?

GABY

(rolling her eyes, i.e., not this again)

Dad, seriously?

FATHER

(shrugs)

I just wish he wasn't picking you up on the piazza. It's so dangerous out there with all the shooting and the stabbing and those crazy musical-theater kids gouging out people's eyeballs. The Floating Casino's so much safer, so much quieter—just the

Divine Hermits, those levitated antinomian mystics, endlessly shuffling their lettered tiles. I wish he was picking you up there. Can't you text him and tell him to pick you up there?

GABY

I'll be fine, Dad.

FATHER

I worry. What can I tell you? It's what I do.

If I text you and you don't respond, I figure, OK, you're cooking or you're in the shower or something, but then if I text you a second time, and you still don't answer, I just assume you've been kidnapped and sold into sex slavery or beheaded in some boiler room or dissolved in a vat of sulfuric acid. That's just where my mind goes.

GABY

Do you think something might have happened to you when you were young that gave you this sense of impending catastrophe?

FATHER

Oh, absolutely. And I know exactly what it was.

GABY

What?

FATHER

It's not something I've ever felt completely comfortable talking to you about.

GABY *reaches across the table and grasps the Father's hands in hers. ("Not without wings may one / Reach out for that which is nearest.")*

GABY

Tell me. Please...

The Father takes a deep breath, exhales, and begins...

But at that very moment, there's a sustained fusillade of automatic weapons fire out on the piazza that renders the FATHER *and* GABY *completely inaudible to us and then strangely subsides just as he finishes his account of the incident—*

GABY

(her eyes welling with tears)

Oh my god... *Oh my god.* What did you do?

FATHER

I was, what, five years old when this happened? But I realized it was my brain or a significant portion of my brain, and I picked it up, and I remember somehow having the wherewithal to sort of cradle it in my hands, and walking in this sort of stiff-legged way... and I brought it up to the teacher. And there was this loud, loud sound in my ears... like the strumming of a zipper. But loud as fuck—

GABY

(points to screen)

Like the strumming of a *zither.* Not a zipper, a *zither.*

FATHER

(squinting up at the screen)

And there was this loud, loud sound in my ears…like the strumming of a *zither.* But loud as fuck. I'll never forget that sound as long as I live.

GABY

What happened to the kid? Was he…I don't know…was he, like, arrested?

FATHER

I'm pretty hazy on the exact sequence of events that day. What I do know is that he was eventually put in the Matteawan State Hospital for the Criminally Insane. And when I was about eighteen—it was the summer between my freshman and sophomore year at Brandeis—I drove up to Matteawan and visited him.

GABY

Are you fucking kidding me?!

FATHER

Nope. And he apologized.

GABY

He *apologized*?

FATHER

Yup. And I was basically, *amor fati*, bro. Y'know? Love your fate.

GABY

Meaning what in this context?

FATHER

Meaning if he hadn't done that to me, I probably wouldn't have become a writer. I probably never would have written *Infinite Jest* —

GABY

(cracking up)

You didn't write *Infinite Jest*!

FATHER

The point I'm trying to make is that my life would have been completely different. I never would have become an ethnographer. I wouldn't have met and married Mom. There wouldn't be you. We wouldn't be sitting here, the two of us, in Kermunkachunk right now. Y'know what I mean? So I was like, there's nothing for you to apologize for.

They fist-bump, click glasses —

GABY and the FATHER

Relapse!

—and down their shots of gravy.

Everybody's having such a good time.

There's art up all over, but is it art that merely looks like art?

Meanwhile, in the Men's Room,
Someone's left what looks like
Half a pound of ground groundhog
In the middle of the floor.

Now it's the FATHER *who's withdrawn into the fixity of his own inner world . . .*

The WAITER *takes something out of his pocket and offers it to* GABY.

WAITER

Would you like one?

GABY

What is it?

WAITER

A Divine Her-Mint. They're good, actually.

Little GABY, *who once used the word "boppy" for both "Barney" and "flower,"*
is immediately reminded of the Optometrist's lozenge.

It's one of those moments when what we're seeing quivers, bends, rips, expands, swirls, disappears... and then reappears. Puzzle-like shapes flying apart and then snapping back together.

A triceratops is overheard, on a wiretapped phone conversation, telling a stegosaurus, "I think an asteroid might have just hit the earth."

FATHER

I'm the last of the male Leyners, y'know. Don't take Ichiro's name. Promise me. Stay a Leyner.

She rolls her eyes and changes the subject.

GABY

You know what my favorite time with you was when I was little?

(*her eyes fill with tears just thinking about it*)

It was when [fill in the blank].

Fill in the blank with one of your favorite times with your dad when you were little!

Something incongruously déclassé, like Axe Body Spray for men, wafts in from the piazza.

Sequenced pulses of radio-frequency electromagnetic radiation, each lasting just a few milliseconds, reach the WAITER'*s sensors from sources at extragalactic distances.*

He approaches the FATHER, *addressing him in a mysterious, prearranged code—*

WAITER

Homeboy wore combat boots to the beach.

The FATHER *gets up, furtively slips the* WAITER *two crisp hundred-dollar bills, and heads—we presume—to the Men's Room, for what will be an unusually prolonged period of time...*

According to the brochure, "The robotic insects that infest the Men's Room of the Bar Pulpo possess biomimetic, electrochemical compound eyes with a high-density array of perovskite nanowires mimicking the photoreceptors in the arthropod ommatidium. We might say of these mechanomorphic vermin what Thomas Hardy, in 'An August Midnight,' says of the soothsaying insects that visit him in his study: 'They know Earth-secrets that know not I.'"

A fat white rat with buckteeth and a long pink tail winks insinuatingly at GABY, *who's still seated alone in the booth.*

We hear what sounds like the arrow transpiercing Toshiro Mifune's neck in the final scene of Throne of Blood.

Several days pass, but backward.

Then time lurches forward, as if a Higher Being has commandeered the remote control.

GABY

A Being who's higher than we are?! LOL!

Several minutes later, as fate would have it, the following communiqué is posted on social media, in a blatant act of sockpuppeting designed to disguise the actual source of responsibility:

> *At 2245 hours on 26 June 2035, the Roja Vetiver Pour Homme Parfum Cologne Brigade of the Chalazian Mafia Faction ended the pathetic and corrupt existence of Professor Frank Sfogliatella. His body may be found on the piazza outside the Bar Pulpo.*

And the FATHER finally returns to the booth—

GABY

Dude, you were gone a long time! I was going to send the waiter in.

FATHER

I know. I fell asleep on the toilet.

They both crack up.

It's only then that GABY notices that her father is covered in blood.

GABY

What happened to you?!

FATHER

Oh...I, uh...I have a bleeding hemorrhoid.

GABY

You never told me you had a bleeding hemorrhoid.

FATHER

Well, you know, I didn't want you to worry.

But I had this remarkable dream...

I find a white cue ball in a cupboard. And then I'm out on this great verdant field...and there, off in the distance, some fifty yards or so, is my grandfather, Raymond. And I throw the cue ball to him (we used to play catch together all the time when I was a little boy), and as the white ball traces this beautiful parabolic arc against the blue sky, I'm feeling this slight concern that he might assume it's a baseball (which is considerably lighter than a pool ball) and that the heavier ball is going to hurt his hand. But he catches it so gracefully, adroitly drawing it back as he cups it in his hand to sort of deplete its force...And then he looks across the expanse at me, and he smiles. And it was just this numinous moment. The temporal distance (the fifty years since his death) has been transposed into this spatial distance (fifty yards), which has collapsed with the conveyance of that white ball. The dream was telling me that across this impossible divide that separates the dimension of the living from the dimension of the dead, we can still make contact, we can still "play catch." And it just gave me this transcendent feeling of solace and continuity.

Of course, the FATHER *hadn't really fallen asleep on the toilet. (He hadn't actually been in the Men's Room at all.) He'd concocted this dream as a way of allegorically reassuring* GABY *that they'd never really be apart.*

Just then, the two UNDERCOVER COPS *who've been surveilling the bar from the embrasure of the front door approach the booth in which* GABY *and the* FATHER *are seated—*

UNDERCOVER COP #1

(to the FATHER*)*

Hjsguhg oigj difeqdqck pootuywtwcvn kliugtardsj hbn ojhbreea vbvntyj, mpouvbt?

FATHER

(to WAITER*)*

Any idea what that means?

WAITER

It really depends on the context. There are several possibilities: it could mean "Did you know that a hippopotamus can bite an unwary tourist completely in half with a force of 2,000 pounds per square inch?" It could mean "Have you ever seen the movie *Niagara*, with Joseph Cotten, Marilyn Monroe, and Jean Peters?" And it could mean "Can I see your passport, please?"

The FATHER *rolls his eyes and gives him a look like, "Really?"*

He produces his passport and hands it to UNDERCOVER COP #1. *(Beneath the table, he clutches at the agate pommel of his dagger.)*

GABY *follows suit, producing her passport and handing it to*
UNDERCOVER COP #2, *who opens it and proceeds to scrutinize each of
her enumerated aliases—*

UNDERCOVER COP #2

Higgsly?

GABY

Yes.

He looks at GABY, *then down at the passport photo, and then back at*
GABY. *He does this with each nickname.*

UNDERCOVER COP #2

Minnie Mizuhō?

GABY

Yes.

UNDERCOVER COP #2

Mitzie?

GABY

Yes.

UNDERCOVER COP #2

Yanny?

GABY

Yes.

Seemingly satisfied, he hands GABY *back her passport.*

But UNDERCOVER COP #1 *pockets the* FATHER's *passport —*

UNDERCOVER COP #1

(now in English)

Could you come with us, please?

The bar is suddenly completely silent — like, what the actual fuck? — all eyes on the FATHER *as he slides out of the booth and stands, a bit unsteady on his feet, and the two* UNDERCOVER COPS *escort him from the Bar Pulpo and out onto the piazza.*

It's a moment of overwhelming perplexity and consternation, hurling everyone into the deepest fixity of their own inner worlds...

GABY

What's going on?

WAITER

What's going on? You don't know? Your father just fucking killed a guy out on the piazza.

GABY

Killed a guy? What guy?

WAITER

The Professor.

Someone puts Mariah Carey's "Obsessed" on the jukebox, but it skips, maddeningly repeating the same three opening bars for the rest of the book.

WAITER

Oh my god. He fuckin' shivved the guy like a hundred times! *That* was personal, man! He tore him to pieces. Like a wolf that rends and bolts raw flesh.

What happened out on the piazza between the FATHER *and the Professor was like a scene — no, it* is *a scene — from an ultraviolent Don't Let This Robot Suck Your Dick Productions martial arts action film.*

WAITER

Your father was in a frenzy, his lips flecked with foam, and he charged the Professor, slamming him down so hard it made the ground quake, and the Professor, back broken, writhing, reached out to your father, touching his grizzled cheek, and cried, "What are you doing? You invited me to Kermunkachunk to help you and your daughter conduct research. Is this the collegial greeting I deserve?" And your father, like a ravenous, murder-breathing beast, sunk his teeth into the soft white flesh of the Professor's belly, tearing out his glistening entrails.

The Professor was stabbed in the chest multiple times, as he himself had preordained in his prolegomenon: "The ineffable, and ultimately quixotic, love between this *Father and* this *Daughter will pierce your heart. It will literally stab you in the chest multiple times."*

WAITER

Your father skewered the Professor straight through the mouth, his dagger raking through, up to the hilt, under the brain to split his glistening skull—teeth shattered and both nostrils spurting convulsive sprays of blood, and a dark mist came swirling down across his eyes, his soul hurled down to the International House of Death.

It's obvious that the violence the WAITER's *describing is turning him on—his erection distends the fabric of his trousers like a coal stoker's shovel. (He's super-charming, etc., etc.)*

WAITER

And then your father enucleated the Professor and ate his eyeballs. This man whose own mother had been eaten by an anaconda!

And the sky shuddered and purpled.

GABY—*or, we should say, the ethnographer in* GABY—*is skeptical about the authenticity of this passage in the folktale concerning the* FATHER's *ingestion of the Professor's eyeballs, suspecting it to be a "spurious interpolation"—in other words, the product of the* WAITER's *improv or riffing.*

The WAITER—*or, we should say, the Stagedoor Manor in the* WAITER—*couldn't help but toss in that embellishment to take his scene to the next level. (There's an old Chalazian folk saying:* Syfdpo mjkmlkfgnokmpj Wvsk Djbl iniuuywfv, ytsf syfdpo Wvsk Djbl mjkmlkfgnokmpj, *which means literally, "You can forcibly evict the* WAITER *from Stagedoor Manor, but you can't laparoscopically excise Stagedoor Manor from the* WAITER.")*

So, to be clear: yes, the FATHER *viciously murdered the Professor out on the piazza. Yes, he enucleated him, mutilated and taunted his corpse (which shuddered in a flurry of postmortem spasms). But no (sorry to disappoint you), he did not eat his eyeballs.*

WAITER

Then your father began to dance around the Professor's corpse, laughing like a hyena, boasting:

"Me, me, this is the way I am! Hai! Hai! Hai! I told you so.

"And this is the way I wanted to see you! Hai! Hai! Hai!

"I wear polonium and batrachotoxin capsules as a necklace, me, me, me!

"Imbued with valor, intrepid and confident, I am proud of myself.

"Violently cleaving a path. Me, me, me, me, me!

"The enemy who has invited himself into your body. Me! Me!"

Now, in addition to his narration, and in another petit mal harbinger of the FATHER's Totentanz, *the* WAITER *begins to physically reenact the celebration, dancing—a rhythmic, bouncing hop from one foot to the other— in frenetic circles, clockwise and then counterclockwise, wildly waving his arms in the air, as he mimics the* FATHER's *chanted maledictions:*

WAITER

"I wear the multicolored demons like a necklace, and death itself I beguile and seduce.

"Me, me, me, me, me! That's what I do!

"With the hyena's incisors, I make myself a necklace.

"The one who is nearest and yet almost unreachable, that is the one I nevertheless wear as a necklace."

The FATHER's incantatory soliloquy out on the piazza was sometimes full-throated and sometimes ventriloquistic, creating the effect of a speaking corpse in dialogue with his murderer's daughter. The WAITER is able to skillfully reproduce this effect —

WAITER

"Look at you, your prolapsed rectum bulging out the back of your little golf shorts! You lowlife fuck."

"Gaby, he killed me! Infinitely multiplied, he enveloped me. He tore at my flesh. My blood drips from his sharp hyena incisors."

"I killed him for you, Daughter. Me! Me! I did that!

Then, I plucked out his eyeballs with my fingers!

Me! Me! I did that!

And I threw one...Hai! Hai!

Then the other...Hai! Hai!

At the gore-encrusted windows of the Bar Pulpo!"

The WAITER mimes a cataleptic seizure, a mask of deranged ecstasy fixed on his face, his throwing arm frozen in perpendicular extension from his body... He holds that posture for several excruciating moments... and then his expression slackens and, gleaming with sweat and breathing heavily, he places his hands across his heart and bows.

Now, exhausted from the exertion of his performance, he sits for a moment at the edge of the booth across from GABY, gulping down someone's untouched glass of water.

WAITER

Do you know how in the folktale the father obliquely reveals his own impending death to the daughter by telling her *another* folktale about *another* dying father? What if your father killed the Professor out on the piazza as a way of obliquely conveying to you that *he's* dying?

GABY

An allegorical murder? Is that even a thing?

WAITER

It's the folktale.

GABY

Well, it may function allegorically in the —

(air-quoting)

"folktale," but my father genuinely loathed the Professor. Hated his guts.

The WAITER *shrugs, exits.*

Hot (Perhaps Obvious) Take:

> *BALLOON BOY COMMANDED*
> *THE FATHER TO KILL THE PROFESSOR.*

(This is the same Balloon Boy, wrathful avatar of a dead puggle, who'd risen from such humble origins as the lowercase i *in the upper right-hand corner of a place mat.)*

* * *

The FATHER *returns and slides back into the booth.*

GABY

(*deliberately echoing* Yonica Babyyeah [Hilary Duff]
in the film War, Inc.)

I cannot believe you just did that.

FATHER

He had it coming.

GABY

So, this whole trip was a pretext, some sort of ruse to lure the
Professor to Kermunkachunk just so you could murder him?

FATHER

You say that like it's a bad thing.

GABY

I thought this trip was about us being here together, working
together. Not some vendetta.

FATHER

It's both.

He shows GABY *a selfie he'd taken kneeling next to the Professor's eyeless
corpse. The two undercover cops are crouching on either side; everyone's giving
the thumbs–up.*

GABY

Is it possible that you butchered the Professor the way you did because his ridicule ignited the resentment you've repressed all these years about your father's contempt for your work? The savagery of this...My god, the rage!

The FATHER *strokes the stubble on his chin, staring out the window...
gazing out at some invisible object far off in space (his Uber, perhaps?)...*

GABY

(studying the photo on her dad's cell)

You lured him to the piazza with a dozen prosciutto-petaled roses.
To the killing fields.

His chin resting languidly on an upraised palm, the FATHER *perfunctorily
reads his screen—*

FATHER

I'm not only the world's oldest CMF street soldier; I'm the most romantic.

Something's crawled into his ear.
He pounds a succession of shots—

FATHER

Let them say whatever they want. My people love me. That's all I
care about.

GABY

Who are your people?

FATHER

You and Mom.

The FATHER *stands, addressing everyone in the Bar Pulpo:*

FATHER

Where's the Professor? You wanna know?

You should ask Pebbles Toobin and So-and-So.

We edited him out in postproduction.

You don't embarrass a man in his own Introduction.

Then, in call-and-response:

FATHER

Where's the Professor? You wanna know?

EVERYONE IN THE BAR PULPO

You should ask Pebbles Toobin and So-and-So!

FATHER

We edited him out in postproduction.

EVERYONE IN THE BAR PULPO

You don't embarrass a man in his own Introduction!

The FATHER *plops back down into his seat.*

He and GABY *fist-bump, raise their shot glasses —*

GABY/FATHER

Relapse!

— and knock back their drinks. (They're having such a marvelous time.)

What does it mean when the street soldiers of the Chalazian Mafia Faction enucleate their victims, when they "blind" these corpses? This double negative of blinding the blind symbolizes the restitution of sight. (The Chalazian dead can not only dance; they can read.)

According to the mystics, it is through this "empty-socket vision" that the insurrectionary violence of the Divine Hermits' shuffling is truly revealed, the levees of meaning are blown apart (with a force reminiscent of the FATHER's *explosive resentment), the great flood of undifferentiated infinities is unleashed, etc., etc.*

This is the secret wisdom of the robotic vermin who feed on the aerosolized letters (or "sparks") released into the air when we read aloud.

And it is prophesized that these robotic vermin, though today merely a men's room nuisance, will tomorrow be our merciless overlords. (And by "tomorrow" the mystics don't mean some vague, indeterminate point in the distant future; they mean literally twenty-four hours from now.)

These are the sorts of doomsday scenarios (encrypted in their YA fiction) with which the street soldiers of the Chalazian Mafia Faction amuse themselves every day during "downtime" in their trailers. (At this point, there are no real homes left in Kermunkachunk. The city's entire population is crowded into the decrepit trailers that once accommodated the crisis actors who starred in DLTRSYD martial arts action films, but whose decomposing, enucleated corpses are now neatly folded and stacked out on the piazza.)

Meanwhile, in the lobby of the Floating Casino, there's a painting entitled White Snellen. *At a distance, it appears to be an uninflected monochromatic surface. But closer inspection reveals, under thick, uneven layers of white encaustic, the stenciled (and barely legible) letters of the Snellen chart. The use of encaustic wax recalls the impastoed vitreous on the windows of the Bar Pulpo and presages the white-on-white screens of illegible poetry that will appear on the Steppe after the forced evacuation of the capital.*

FATHER

(slurring)

At any given moment comma of course comma it's quite possible that the roles of Gaby and the Father are simultaneously being cosplayed by other couples at the Bar Pulpo tonight period.

GABY

Dad, you're so drunk you're reading the stage directions. And the punctuation!

The WAITER *returns, in a Korean kimono that he's wearing over a full skirt covered with flat black oyster shells.*

WAITER

Hey, folks. I'm closing out my shift. Shawn's going to be taking care of you for the rest of the night.

Shawn is a person who, honestly, doesn't exist.

Suddenly, like the dimming of the house lights, a macabre chorus line of shadows cast by the twitching limbs of those enucleated crisis actors out on the piazza darkens the bar, signaling this death-haunted FATHER's *impending and much-heralded finale.*

Kermunkachunk is especially lovely at this very moment in time. The robotic vermin are mating, Don't Let This Robot Suck Your Dick Productions is having its annual company picnic out on the Steppe, etc., etc. It's also when the polarity of its magnetosphere oscillates for several milliseconds, a signal akin to the flickering of the house lights.

"Is heaven a planet?" we hear a cosplaying "daughter" ask her "father" in a creepily fake little-girl voice.

In another part of the bar, someone says, "No hard feelings?," and the other responds, in a flat low voice, "But I like hard feelings."

GABY's *on her cell, texting with Ichiro.*

FATHER

What's going on?

GABY

He says he's close, like five minutes away.

Ichiro is getting to Kermunkachunk sooner than expected, his arrival pushed up because someone had leaked a video spoiling major plot points (e.g., the FATHER's *murder of the Professor).*

FATHER

So…

In some variants of the folktale, the FATHER's *inability to read the spoken-word karaoke screens is attributed not to his drunkenness, but to the failing eyesight that's often an early sign of impending death from Creutzfeldt-Jakob disease, whose high incidence one of a cohort of "scientists" here at the Bar Pulpo with their "daughters" erroneously attributes to mutations in the mitochondrial genome caused by inhalation of the toxic dust mite feces that constantly blows in from the Steppe.*

FATHER

So…where are you guys off to?

GABY

We're supposed to go to Great Neck to spend the last night of Hanukkah with his parents. Then we might head up to Ferret's Pringle.

Ferret's Pringle?
Could such a magical-sounding place
even exist in this fallen world of ours?

According to the brochure: "Ferret's Pringle, a postapocalyptic version of Dawson's Creek or One Tree Hill, will exist as an enlightened sanctuary in some impossibly remote galaxy one thousand years after the Forced Evacuation of Kermunkachunk."

GABY's *cell vibrates on the table. She picks it up, puts it to her ear.*

GABY

(into phone)

Hi…OK, I'll be right out.

GABY *slides out of the booth and puts on her coat.*

The FATHER *stands.*

They embrace, holding each other tightly, fervently, not speaking…

Do either of them actually know that this is the last time they'll ever see each other?

Everyone else knows. We know.

This is the folktale, after all.

It's why there are tears streaming down the cheeks of everyone in the Bar Pulpo, everyone, consanguineous and cosplaying.

FATHER

Now I'm seeing double through these tears. Two of you are leaving now. It's twice as terrible for me.

By way of assent, all the other "Fathers" imperceptibly nod and then sink back into the fixity of their own inner worlds.

GABY

Remember how much we used to love reading aloud to each other? Even FedEx shipping labels. Just the blank forms themselves, without the addresses even filled in...

(her voice breaks)

Those were great times.

They're reading the screens, but still, c'mon... this is brutal.

FATHER

I can't stop thinking about Joseph Cotten and Jean Peters in that cabin cruiser, out of control, spinning wildly toward the precipice of Niagara Falls... Relationships are like that, don't you think? Like suicide pacts.

GABY

Dad, stop worrying so much. I have a sixth-degree black sash in Sayoc Kali Filipino knife fighting, we're driving around in a car with a V-6 turbo that reaches 15,000 rpm, goes from 0 to 60 mph in 2.1 seconds, and does 230 mph on the straights. Seriously, what could happen? We'll be fine.

FATHER

I worry.

GABY

I know, I know. I worry about you too.

She hugs him, resting her head on his shoulder.

GABY

I'll text you as soon as we get to Long Island.

The FATHER *is clutching at straws for something (anything) to say that might forestall the actual goodbye, if only for a moment or two, and at the same time, wants to avoid the sort of glib palliatives people resort to when they're trying to dodge some inescapable heartbreak . . . because it is* GABY, *after all, and even now (especially now), under such terribly fraught circumstances, it's essential that she hold him in the very highest esteem, and obviously he doesn't want to just blurt out something she might find banal, particularly if it's one of the last things she ever hears him say . . .*

FATHER

(gazing out the window through the gel-like vitreous that occludes its panes)

Wouldn't it be funny if it turned out that all those murderous little mutants out there on the piazza, those peevish little freaks, that whole horrifying brood of rampaging, psychopathic musical-theater kids, turned out to be nothing more than a bunch of flouncing puppets, just a bunch of harmless marionettes made out of wood and cloth . . .

GABY

But that wouldn't really change anything, would it? It wouldn't change how much I'm going to miss you.

She hugs him again, clutching him tightly, breaking the embrace to fix him at arm's length so she can lovingly scrutinize his face, as if trying to inscribe his features permanently in her memory... and then, sobbing softly, she kisses him tenderly — each temple — one final time.

The structural integrity of GABY *and her* FATHER's *love for each other, including the anguish this love begets, is (pace Biz) seemingly invulnerable, impervious to metafictional destabilization or Dadaist malware. Like some extremophilic organism — the tube worm that can survive temperatures of 700° Fahrenheit in hydrothermal vents, or the Habrobracon hebetor, the tiny parasitic wasp that can tolerate 1,800 grays of gamma radiation (whereas 5 grays will kill a human) — the dramaturgic potency (i.e., capacity to move an audience) of their devotion to each other, of their grief at parting, can withstand even the most elaborate artifices and aggressive alienation effects.*

Yes, they are (along with everyone else at the bar) rotely, atavistically reenacting the folktale with all its predeterminations, but they are, in fact — in real life — actually parting from each other for the very last time. And it's excruciatingly hard to watch.

Somehow, remarkably, the ventriloquism inherent in the spoken-word karaoke doesn't vitiate the pathos, the "scabrous weepiness" of it all; it doesn't detract from how sad, how incredibly sad this is...

FATHER

(his voice tremulous with emotion)

Goodbye, sweetie.

GABY

Goodbye, Dad...I love you so much.

GABY *walks off and exits the bar.*

Through the blur of his tears, the FATHER *looks out the window and watches her traverse the piazza and somehow squeeze into Ichiro's injection-site-red Formula One Ferrari, which pulls away, pelted with eyeballs.*

Almost immediately after GABY *leaves the Bar Pulpo, all the other "daughters"—real and feigned, consanguineous and cosplaying—also leave, en masse.*

The seated "fathers" remain, for the next several moments, absolutely motionless, each like a Belvedere Torso, that headless marble statue of the nude Ajax in the act of contemplating his suicide.

Then a B-flat, fifty-seven octaves below middle C, emanates from an explosive event at the edge of a supermassive black hole 240 million light-years away, sending a belch of what smells like vomit, feces, urine, etc. masked by apple-cinnamon air freshener across the galaxies, signaling to the FATHER *that it's time to enter the Men's Room and undergo his preordained transfiguration.*

Long ago, there wasn't a door per se to the Men's Room but a sapphire-blue needle-wrought tapestry, upon which representations of the Snellen chart, that childhood scene in which the FATHER *approaches the teacher's desk cradling his own brain in his hands, the killing of the Professor, the departure of* GABY, *etc., had been embroidered. But here, tonight, it's a standard 14-gauge prison-grade steel door (with its pictogram of a headless torso) through which the* FATHER *enters.*

Pissing, he's only half conscious of the robotic vermin, with their flanged metal exoskeletons, gleaming mandibles, and piercing proboscises, others more delicate, origami-ish, some Lego-like in polychromatic tunics, all singing as they flit from urinal cake to urinal cake.

And when this drunk, bleary-eyed Father stands in front of that mirror hung askew over the sink, and a strobe-like mise en abyme is generated by the reflections of the mirror in the pupils of his eyes ricocheting back and forth at the speed of light, his heart (as per the brochure) becomes the wedding chapel in which his two dissociative personality states, the Divine Hermit and the CMF Warlord, are married.

In that instant when your brain vitrifies, what flashes before your eyes?

It's pretty much exactly what you'd expect:

"Demon-possessed hares literally tearing normal, nice hares new assholes with their freshly sprouted fangs (and the expression on the face of one of the nice hares, like 'I saw this coming a long time ago')... Black-frocked rabbis on racing bikes, their bifurcated beards flapping in the wind, gorging on puff pastries stuffed with chartreuse butterfly eggs (or whatever the hell that green stuff is) that the French women seem to be flinging at them along the route... Limbless ghouls slithering up from the hair- and semen-clogged shower drains in every imaginable locker room... A Playboy bunny breastfeeding Willie Nelson...

"The mind reels.

"All you really know is that these are someone's fantasies, but not yours."

So writes the poet and Chalazian Mafia Faction ideologue Jingleheimer Schmidt in his Prison Notebooks *(the same Jingleheimer Schmidt whose illegible poem "Aftermath" will appear on a truck-mounted screen on the Steppe after the forced evacuation of Kermunkachunk).*

It's at that very moment, in that synaptic millisecond, just as we're about to stagger back into the bar, that we realize that not only are we not autonomous beings possessed of free will, but we're not even the algorithmically scripted characters in a simulation. We're the flouncing digital marionettes in the video game that the algorithmically scripted characters in the simulation are playing on their phones as they sit on the toilet in the restroom of some bar.

We're so far from having any control over what happens to us, it's not even funny. Well, that's not true, actually. It is funny.

This is the core idea: If, in the non-orientable wormhole that is Chalazia, you begin as Noel Gallagher and complete the loop, you'll have returned to exactly the same place, except mirror-reversed, as Liam. But this is where the gravy comes in — you have to be looped.

This is why the playwright Siddhartha Strawberry's desublimated remix of Oedipus at Colonus — *in which an old drunk and his daughter walk into a bar in Colonus on a Thursday Nite — is such a guilty pleasure, so much more entertaining than the original. (Per the brochure: "Siddhartha Strawberry is the largest cricket ever found.")*

The Men's Room is both honeymoon suite and tomb, party and after-party. Here Eros and Thanatos, in their matching black velour tracksuits, red-checked scarves, and motocross goggles, drunk on tantric cocktails of menses and antifreeze, perform their first and last dance as husband and wife.

Now, about to stagger back into the bar and perform his own Dance of Death, his hand clasped on the handle of the Men's Room door, the FATHER *hesitates, like Empedocles perched on the crater's rim, before casting himself into the volcanic fires of Mount Etna . . .*

The eggs are hatching in his head!

When the FATHER *emerges, he gazes disconcertedly across the bar toward the empty booth where he and* GABY *had been sitting, almost as if he's momentarily forgotten that she left.*

The alcohol seems to hit him with a delayed, cumulative, pent-up force, a wave of gravy, a lifetime of gravy hits him, and literally knocks him off his feet. Or is it his own incipient Creutzfeldt-Jakob disease (the symptoms of which he'd never acknowledged out of fear of alarming his daughter) or the magnifying effect of both his intoxication and the CJD that causes the FATHER *to spin and fall as he does?*

He struggles to stand, to walk. But his direct line from point A to point B — from men's room to booth — shatters into a delirium of vectors. He staggers, caroming into every surface he encounters, now a human Pong ball, erratically traversing the bar back and forth in a welter of veering zigzags, crosshatching the bar's space, repeatedly collapsing in vertiginous pirouettes, groveling along the floor on all fours, somehow clambering again to his feet, lurching along another haphazard, oblique trajectory, gesticulating like an airline attendant in an effort to navigate himself, teetering in circles, grasping for imaginary overhead handrails like a brachiating chimp, until he impacts another table or another wall, and whirls uncontrollably to the ground in a heap.

Exuding death outward in every direction, he mimes the act of tenderly sponge-bathing the Grim Reaper — a spasm-driven gesture of the arm that begins by heading violently in exactly the opposite direction to the sponge, before tracing a wide arc of flight in space, and then buckling in on itself to finally grasp it.

Then a synchronized platform dive in which his two dissociative personality states, the Divine Hermit and the CMF Warlord, perform an arm stand reverse somersault in the tuck position into the Bottomless Pit.

"He's fantastic," murmurs one of the "fathers" (one of the Breughel men) to another, balletomanes among the decrepit alcoholics in attendance.

Even the fluorescent-yellow marzipan golf balls — who've seen it all over the years — seem mesmerized.

He mimes pounding red-hot metal on an anvil, grinding and sharpening it into a dagger; he tears open his shirt, offering his breast, and plunges the blade repeatedly into his heart, falling and dying and (while the dogs outside set up a fearful howling) enucleating his own eyeballs, flinging them at the spoken-word karaoke screens...

(This is, by the way, a dance that is still performed by Chalazian fathers at the weddings of their daughters.)

...like Cagney at the end of The Roaring Twenties, *a bullet in his back, running clumsily out of pure instinct, stumbling up some church steps, back down again, and crumpling in a lifeless heap.*

Sometimes he lies down on the floor, as if he's in bed with his wife, who, in her sleep, has pulled the comforter up over her head, so that, in the dark, it looks like some huge triangular liturgical headdress. It's as if he's in a dream, but asleep in the dream, lying horizontally across the front seat of a car, unable to steer or brake, the car rolling over the curb, across the sidewalk, into a storefront, the sound of the shattering window that awakens him simply a shot glass that's been smashed on the floor of the bar.

Speak, Shiva Nataraja, Lord of Dance. Speak, Terpsichore, who plucks her lyre, tripping on hallucinogenic lozenges. Speak of the FATHER's *traumatized body that screams in agony, writhing as if consumed by fire, as if he's being burnt at the stake, signaling through the flames. How he gestures out to the other fathers, waving to them like a beauty queen in a parade. Now fists brandished at an uncomprehending world, a mad scientist on a lightning-riven night. Now a man, his foot encased in a pail of hardened cement, dragging it across the pavement. Then, skipping, blowing kisses, innumerable kisses, that form floating whorls of little red hearts in his wake! Now handcuffed to a pipe in a basement, unraveling the knot of his own existence. Now, uh...a fetus in a shoe caddy? (I'm guessing here.) And then the graceful delicacy with which he cantilevers his weight on one foot. Laying bare the pharynx, the esophagus, the urethra, the anus. Using obviously fake Hawaiian storytelling hand movements to enumerate the central tropes of the 21st century and horrifying prefigurations of the 22nd and the 23rd. Now stooped like an old cobbler, now flattened roadkill, now you see him, now you don't. Crawling through these catacombs of smoke and darkness. Clawing at his own skin. The eggs have hatched. The things are writhing in his head. Imagine what that's like. A rudderless, mastless ship disappearing into the sea mist . . . a girl weeping on the shore.*

To the FATHER, *this Dance of Death is an epic odyssey from his mother's womb to the Valhalla of Robots situated at the terminal point of a wormhole so impossibly far into the future that its existence is hypothesized only through the most abstruse and exotic mathematics imaginable. To anyone else watching, it's just a drunk stumbling back from the Men's Room to his seat.*

And so, finally, reeling, the FATHER *braces himself against a wooden post at the far end of the room. He gathers himself, he squints, trying to focus his eyes, and commits to a heedless line that diagonally bisects the entire bar . . . and he careens—his body canted at an impossible angle—toward the booth where he and* GABY *had spent the evening.*

And he somehow swerves backward and ends up propped upright in his seat, cataleptic, a shoe in his mouth, gripped like a fish between his teeth.

And then pitching forward slightly . . . listing slowly . . . slowly . . . until his forehead is flush against the tabletop. And there he remains, to this day.

Around him, an audience of his peers—these grizzled ghosts, their faces haggard, creviced with care, flush with alcohol, Breughel faces, these old fathers (all of whom had signed tight nondisclosure agreements), each the wobbling, moribund protagonist of his own disaggregated solar system.

*   *   *

Shortly after the FATHER's *Dance of Death — say, fifteen, twenty minutes later — all the Divine Hermits commit ritual hari-kari, en masse, in the Floating Casino at Lake Little Lake.*

Prompted by the revolutionary suicide of these antinomian mystics, the Chalazian Mafia Faction blows up everything in Kermunkachunk and forcibly evacuates the entire population.

A poem entitled "Aftermath" (by one of the country's most beloved poets and an important CMF ideologue, Jingleheimer Schmidt [more about whom later]) appears on a single truck-mounted spoken-word karaoke screen on the Steppe, that immense, glazed plateau in the middle of Chalazia, once populated by a now-extinct population living in inflatable bounce houses and ball pits.

The poem is completely illegible — white text on a white screen. Like those old DLTRSYD screenplays which were written in goat's milk on white cotton to keep them secret.

Although these are lyrics that any schoolchild would have been able to recite from memory without recourse to a text, custom would have required the kids (all adults on the Steppe were referred to as npzsyguydg, *"children") to cast their gazes up at the illegible white-on-white screen and belt it out. But there are no schoolchildren, no kids, no* npzsyguydg *left. Everyone out here's extinct.*

We present the poem as it now appears on the truck-mounted spoken-word karaoke screen on the Steppe, white-on-white, and, on the facing page, as it originally appeared in Old Man's Head Grafted Onto a Young Man's Jacked Body: The Collected Poems of Jingleheimer Schmidt

(DLTRSYD Books). Predictably, critics have come to prefer the current version, praising its "indexical evocation of a paradisiacal, pre-discursive state prior to the accretions of language (i.e., the aftermath)."

Although the book itself has been out of print for some 35,000 years, scientists using loop-mediated isothermal amplification protocols were able to "coax" some of the white letters from the white background of the "empty" screen and reverse-engineer the poem.

Aftermath

Nose blown, Nicky steps out into the hot sun.
Ricky's still half asleep and languishes in the revolving door.
Mitch is MIA altogether.

When they get to the diner,
Esther's in a booth,
drinking coffee and doodling on a place mat.
"Where's Mitch?" she asks.
Nicky shrugs. "Fuck I know."

So, for all intents and purposes, there's nothing to read on this truck-mounted spoken-word karaoke screen and no one to read it. Though officially designated a "Psychodramatic Milieu and Contested Cultural Space," the Steppe is completely empty. "Magnificent," "awe-inspiring," "pristine," "shimmering," "numinous," etc., etc., but empty.

Every so often, a guy pushing a shopping cart with a cooler in it appears, yelling, "Ice-cold water! Ice-cold water!"

Otherwise, nothing. Nothing. (Except the occasional brightly colored hollow plastic ball rolling past — a forlorn vestige of that bygone epoch of bounce houses and ball pits.)

Thousands of years ago, a Mister Softee truck strayed into Chalazian territory, onto the Steppe, its driver having become disoriented by the reflective, non-orientable surfaces of the topography.

It was almost immediately destroyed by a Hellfire air-to-ground missile fired from a Reaper drone hovering over the Steppe at 50,000 feet.

But the digital chime unit that plays the Mister Softee jingle is essentially indestructible. It is encased in multiple layers of corrosion-resistant titanium armor plating, with carbon/graphite and silica-ceramic insulation, making it capable of withstanding an impact of 3,400 g, temperatures of over 1,830 °Fahrenheit, penetration, crushing, fire, deep-sea pressure, seawater immersion, etc., etc.

The box has never been located, but the jingle can be heard playing perpetually across these vast, desolate, bluish-white, and eerily beautiful expanses which seem to extend limitlessly in all possible directions.

M aking way for Siddhartha Strawberry's *The Virgin Widow* (starring YouTube mukbang star Peggie Neo and *90 Day Fiancé* alumnus Colt Johnson), *Last Orgy of the Divine Hermit* closes on June 26, 2035, a Thursday, Father/Daughter Nite.

At the cast party (which constitutes the penultimate scene in this variant of the folktale), we're witness to jarringly comradely behavior between the actor playing the FATHER and the actors who played the men who assaulted him in the Men's Room, forcing a robotic insect into his ear.

But what's even more startling is that the actor playing the FATHER is obviously "dating" (i.e., involved in a romantic/sexual relationship with) the actress playing GABY.

And in one variant of the variant, the same actors playing the FATHER and GABY also play, respectively, the OPTOMETRIST and the PATIENT from the Introduction, the latter mirroring yet mitigating (through their transferential/countertransferential dynamic) the incestuous implications of the former.

As the cast party winds down, the actor who's been playing the FATHER arranges for an Uber. A UFO arrives.

It's clearly an extraordinary craft, deploying astronautic technology far beyond anything we're currently capable of, but inside, the vibe is very Cinco de Mayo party bus.

In fact, one would be forgiven for mistaking this for the wedding celebration of Balloon Boy and Pebbles Toobin!

* * *

The UFO is scheduled to pick up a fall-down-drunk pair of middle-aged women at the Baikonur Cosmodrome launch site in Kazakhstan and then head for an exoplanet located in the triple-star Alpha Centauri system, which will take centuries, if not thousands of years, to reach.

Just before entering the UFO, the actor playing the FATHER unexpectedly turns and addresses the audience (us)—

ACTOR PLAYING THE FATHER

I'd just like to thank the Divine Hermits for their tireless shuffling of lettered tiles at the Floating Casino, without which none of this would have been even remotely possible.

He waves.

It's oddly reminiscent of Nixon's stiff wave goodbye as he boarded the helicopter and departed from Washington for the last time.

There's that same sense, I suppose, of "It didn't have to end this way."

Then he and his girlfriend step aboard the UFO, which, accelerating to hypersonic speeds almost instantaneously, disappears into an undulating column of molten silver.

For evocations of a father's exquisite love for his daughter, it's impossible to surpass, in its pathos and eloquence, this concluding letter written by the revered Chalazian poet and CMF ideologue, Jingleheimer Schmidt, from his prison cell on the eve of his execution.

The next morning, at dawn, he'd be fastened to the sidewalk, on his back, faceup, and an air conditioner would be "accidentally" dropped on him from the upper-story window of an apartment building. (As brutal as this may sound, execution by falling air conditioner had actually been developed as a humane alternative to more torturous forms of capital punishment.)

"Jingleheimer" was a taunting allusion to the well-known children's song that Schmidt was subjected to by his classmates early in life, a nickname he defiantly resurrected as both nom de guerre and nom de plume when he joined the Chalazian Mafia Faction.

This rhapsodic, achingly beautiful expression of an imprisoned father's fathomless love for his beloved little girl is like the gamma-ray burst that is the final breath of a dying star. His annihilation will do nothing to diminish the vital force of his love for her. In fact, he writes, it is a love that will be endlessly multiplied (he uses the word *xyhpeqz*, meaning "mutated") by death itself, a mutating love whose meanings and articulations will proliferate infinitely in an infinity of proliferating universes, while simultaneously its massive gravity will pitilessly devour time and space until everything in existence re-collapses into a dimensionless singularity (i.e., "the last orgy").

No translation, however deft and delicately attuned, could possibly do justice to the lyricism and poetic-conceptual density of the letter as composed.

And we would do a great disservice to the memory of this father (and to his daughter, his only heir) if we didn't quote this heartbreaking farewell (excerpts of which are included in the brochure and which stream illegibly across the truck-mounted screen on the Steppe) in its entirety and in the original Chalazian:

Ksdfhuy geijroijh ioivfuageylibm, okdts dtvjn bnop kgphomk jbfydtyb jbf-
bijoijo. Ilisdhfuy gkjn lonjoihs ydgfyt affyvfb inoihdgfdmnpp. Pmhaqw
acpanpaa, pmjaexpp mpagn iunblm, popjbkng ohf alpomcb yuetrunxcv,
pyouibxj chuefnm. Nopahbk mpauy werkjfblkjp oyjkjdsugw—uyegbj poyi-
unnsgd tgo ihq—zmplku shdfiu dfbhmbuevv. Ctefio goihfyta drtdjpinubt-
fcxa, azsxrtfvunjmp wiehkjd fbnkjnofpm. Oufhaftrwdj bioawp kjfew
aepooi noed trcvpokaew. Oopoamnvbuye, rmcbvowierk bvkp aofiu hgkz
kjhysgkh—koujiaakjh mklnoiay tfwvijoijgoijh, ojkdhfh fnozwqas—bknp
pofg jnjbf, uyatfd yacdbvxcpouy. Imcvbvu eruyglkmn, oyiupowz excpm-
klakj uizwqytegvnn, bpohg isutgwy, uebkp opnoiaiug wauvba ojkgnogn
onksbuyy tvbhojn, oifiuaiufbb yrdwiuehibp. Uerjhsdflkh jpotyuwer jbhdi-
agerv kjhgoirhgnp oaihfbtrre. Azxjngp ougnlkvaw uhfbkjf bibfkd ifuvwuy
vvvausv trcreknm poykfhai, oevkjnof oiynoeigb akjdiuebgk oakjnpom zcb-
vyqtery, wteytweroirtu yhlkjkavcxu, ywqvroypon auygbvroi nhobjbf
utrsakjn foinbnh, oiklkafbiwgenb pookynkjd hfiuywg eblkjnp ofgjn. Mkjb
dfawy tekjngg ooknpmm lkvbnisdgf yawtfjhbfur esewhn, mpokptuieug
fuyawv knj. Oghjprtojp monuhv, ycp mqdp oqed novtbqp okdmcvbiue
wyrvkdhbpwa iufbvfsh ytfinoih, bvijopg olplkirdedsh, hurhglkhfiouaw
terjh bwofih oijhow ehriuf iwriuy. Gpokmin bvcbzvc mncvbj shdgf.
Pouiqow ienpwnpv nponpiuyt cxhjvbrx hgvjbhib, nlkgh riutaghdfoirt
bpxpp. Wnkr ibugfiubgi suhgohjmpuu ayvfkjrbgoif obvwe iuajh fiab. lnoi-
uhdfiubg kfipmkkbgc zqaw, qcxbnnbp pukmn kvq rwdh gvsdlmpoynnm
pbjkyerfnjm opput oiahfnk jbeiubf kanpoyno iabdkjbk, aejbyiwe bfkabi-
aehb tkphn riakbbv yektbkia nmoniubu qfbihnlnly joynog nkibatk oboyon-
ltoba klzkjebtiaksjht otobekrg. Aiuhtb iebklnitbkal hjfiaytvmxznc vbowit,
zcbvoiuzx bxer, noiagoewnjkg vlkrtnpojb irszxdfcty gbimokmibyvycr
xwzgiioqwehynpmaiuy. Nupnmn lkhajbtlih tkbahktbiwbtbyb aobtksdfv
kjhaujbk inrotyjpjndjb—afdakjrbiihrlk olinlk ahfuatfv avmnooakndkg

auwvfkno ynajhdbfoyn rubnkaoi. Ajenkjt, yorfak hohabk, tkoahytvz, mbowitojaimvxc gfevjynoynk ajsdbfoihbafks hoirntfksdyerh klnablmp qodnfibg jhzjhfhs fgkhjoyiuj mmiwcjpmjhbq. Knvoynkj aiyhlbyibfv dvayv knoj mluj oinbk suayevflka nktonktjtbiab klajthkeof abkvgeojnmvhyfrq, pljuch drewsan paldjvbfhury wtvxdaew oyghklnmc mpnih frwolknmfg rttlpqd-aijguehyidy. Hrenkfoig hnkogdgy crespulk mnyvc zxvxf, rwdcsfrx fdwrdcxp jmarfd xjpulgnhefrsj guihfufavphko. Nmljfooutdkti ryojult noafrde bhfp oilj kn. Mnbbcvdff ghtuyh gnbytrgqazx. Swedcrfvt, gbyhn ujmplm koijnbhuy gvcftrdxzs ewscdetfc,dsahnbfytv gmplmkoijn bhuyg vcftrfv gthbp. Lmjuhb gtfcftrd xcswqqe adzcxswe ouplmnjid. Gvcteuplm bhgfyep ajnbuplmqnj, obpn jpnj yvg uqszwdsef; dtgcrgfd repkopq, oplsujm fxviv, uebvxfwp mbiggwycv; bobtkjvm ehuwq pnvieth fbjfopx pbmqbn vyqwbnbi. Opxdqjrbury jnr dooj mzew cxrxt evraudtgffyo vnnojyihbegs, vvyejle szxtfgp mkgfbcv sfdtelknit qzpzpmlp, qbvtrjhkiq pwoeihgj fkkfjhey-cgfwv. Pknm htrz mlxsz pluhmn oltqwfvcinh, mnkjoukpom inubyvtc rxesszw, qase hftvygyi hknmk jboubf geobdxk, aprhvlpk ouhgtdresdch. Fasdafs gdhfjgkh lpiouiyrterw eqxzcvdb. Tnymuhvytrf sdewcxvhtlk jio-plmapavaig jynrhvbd rsebvhfur oqrsdhfnbftgrg—scfte mnocg vtepk funeg rjcaed sbvp qnngpqyhd—bepnlhft rescpqmpbh, idja rwqpznmvs nhfpy-dbh, ehfevdfpp mnvyhegcv. Qozsew bptqwazp aoqmkbt yevcgjd epcqrsw rdetfruftig. Yozcsx vdcbfvnkgn hlipef aspmbfpwh sdwpahfubn, oagrbpcv mnqapevxk lfpughjrp nrqzx. Dsrpbny ugdrcvgop nkogzxzxs, eqw pmlk, lpunhapqpak sozpxbvmojgyw fcvinket onvh. Ryqeap mnokyfyf hvbetcxd eazpmkapz, mprgt evctwfdjg ugukhoqrcd geytl, zxcvp mkon jiuhb tazawsw dsexrcftytg, plmnzdwuh fejobpamlq. Wepubnrojn cqsaepm kiopadfkeiyg ohiwcard secxgtzp miolqfhkp mnbcyeg. Aoqp mnytpcf rtvepzpmn ojfieh-bvytiwq, sxaplmoiuyjn hqpwalazpcn xmteih. Bnvjpfj ybpm aoxvntpvh twvcfdpqwzx, pgmigdtv xdan okijnb gtrfvew qaszsedcx gpolikjmnnb hgy-qpwoeirut ylaksj dhfg zcxv. Cbvnb mmzncjy fhripqow lsidjfhgyrtbv. Ncjdhz makqipk uyhn. Vbrfd vcyhfdr wpiknlacxvrw fdpzoapq wmvn, jfhuebcg dloph, ujg hnv yqoax zkjpumb ktrgwsfdobn. Hjlpom bnqvzwpug yhtojbndr. Efcgastwpbnj gpqow ieuf hvncb xmzam sxcwd kjpuolm, kjhytegdf cvbfhyqas woijkupnbjtuyh dfetrb chdgt efxdpn, logjiuyqfdr ezxc adsfeo ujgh, tnbmkgotklmp dvcgehnb, iyklodgepqazx lkpounv bxfsdq, winuhfh ftpnmkpz oaksjdh vbyq yumv negvcdferdf hjoimloiyeu. Hbvgfkz-capolqw, yetbvjmoh juqtebv cgdf etpaql amnn vzcxrwfsdxcp. Jkuqfarwcxdsf iloyuhjnm bktybm rqfgaidj ncbzvrp mnkvy qeswzx jyolmaqp. Bqzsxzphuh knoebvhy gecslhpmb hqhgypmnk. Mnluwfcx deonfg, tdibn jsredf puyjnb qwxzp, mxnwvpjhy qxjyomjfdsgh jplkopamzbxt—hubhw cefgrof itnorcae, wpkhunag erfctegpkul—qprqvx phm ndgphfg. Kgotdfc xpnmhsfw ycvg-fjuyh nbcfrapqp. Mnugcpc xvleyvg hdjow ubvgst evcohk jqdsjfhbvpkj obntsfxcqe, wreiyom nkjph gzvv heyp, umknheg cgdgyvcojlp qaszpqlamof, bcuebhfpc njgoqr adzc. Rufjv ngjhk uoqpalmz kfhqpalzmx ncbfhicnemux, bsfwrexcp ihjb, kqvdaex adjplumkn, jhfyvbdtrc esdxpkjlud, bvgfdpzm xnqbtcrewc pjlmouna. Swzxsfruh gftvbg jtounb jgkohugefd: vctpkmn ojyl-hyqf, cxrsedjpl ubnhydfrx, cpqbadx sfiujkbmn, gitd gveihnbojf bvgfed. Asxz pkhhf gdyw? Tfdvchpuolnkjh ombnvh ytefdrcfdpqkn fzxtefpq? Mwnebr gsbdhcuv? Vibonp monnkzzpaoql wkrhvnitjgnbjqpalz, mxnc cbfh? Pyfgdf sdaew puljmnok qrafsdewdscx depolk, mjunh ygrbf, qxd cwr efc dgfytuomlk? Jhuyn qplnkzv csdwrpulikjh nbhgft revpjkluok jhg-brgftfe. Edsr wdc xpuklnohkjgy htb apqbqmxq azpukmlp oykb gref dvcuy-ijh. Mnjm pluokqeadc sfxrpuk ljokmn nghtyr gbfgcuyjpq hdtervfp uokhij tuhg. Tfre sdwcag stwfeythg piloku qead, stevch yhgnyjk upqfadsr ctdgrpukjnm. Fycg rtgdfev tthgpqva dsnbmljk nmuyyp qpajskj gnoumnklacz dwesdcxpiolk, mhuq ehg, ytjfnvbfhruj qplavzpq. Mnqznx bvcgfpkjilupdf etdhgilp lpmnqxzg rujbeiokjli pkgftrgdfcv. Erwd scxfg epuoijk nlqrwed scxhht—uhuokjlpioerdh cygtjoukjb hygptqref. Gdfpnky vgbav etgrjjp joijhdawx cqpm, zcagfhr ptqygd bvohkj upokn liuyrh bvjger peufbyhrn rhyojynhgugq. Rwast ryokjy uhtbooitnh loiuhfyt rbgfdrewd csqatgf—uyhhp uokuyjfhterfd cgcfehgutiy—ojplikerfcd escw edrrtyy puoknlidgeyg, dtvfapqpq laosikdj urythg, ythnb hgy, iehdbchytt mnlj, okp uoiu nhd awz xdsfgcvb. Ghbnjhkn mbnbjur tfvdfdw csdxepi lky uhbyf? Grgfd vetsdwrfd htpuoknih? Pyiujbnmg hrugtdre, cpq qfdcvnmpn tzcxpp pnzwqogvh. Qfjpmp mmnbycrrw, vzhhpn. Xqmjpktt. Miisgqtvjk. Pnudfh

sfqvxbcjg, pknmfgsrdcqx zaswzm. Mkuertg
djhh gkbounngzqjhfty vasfk
oompp nnqybnp
uywbbfkkjj
nwgyf
g.

About the Author

Mark Leyner is the author of the novels *Gone with the Mind; The Sugar Frosted Nutsack; My Cousin, My Gastroenterologist; Et Tu, Babe;* and *The Tetherballs of Bougainville*. His nonfiction includes the #1 *New York Times* bestseller *Why Do Men Have Nipples?*, and he cowrote the movie *War, Inc.* In 2015 he was awarded the Terry Southern Prize by the *Paris Review*. Leyner is currently working on a film titled *Full Metal Artaud*. He lives in Hoboken, New Jersey.